Dancers
in the Wind

Dancers
in the Wind

by ANNE COATES

URBANE
Publications

urbanepublications.com

First published in Great Britain in 2016
by Urbane Publications Ltd
Suite 3, Brown Europe House, 33/34 Gleaming Wood Drive,
Chatham, Kent ME5 8RZ
Copyright ©Anne Coates, 2016

A CIP catalogue record for this book is available
from the British Library.

ISBN 978-1-911129-63-9
EPUB 978-1-911129-64-6
MOBI 978-1-911129-65-3

Design and Typeset by Michelle Morgan

Cover by Julie Martin

Printed and bound by CPI Group (UK) Ltd, Croydon, CR0 4YY

urbanepublications.com

The publisher supports the Forest Stewardship Council® (FSC®), the leading international forest-certification organisation.
This book is made from acid-free paper from an FSC®-certified provider. FSC is the only forest-certification scheme
supported by the leading environmental organisations, including Greenpeace.

To Carolyn —
in memory of a great
Vanguard Roadtrips!

Best wishes
Anne

For my lovely daughter, Olivia.

I can enjoy her while she's kind:
But when she dances in the wind,
And shakes her wings and will not stay,
I puff the prostitute away.

John Dryden

ONE

Death might be an equaliser but dying has its own hierarchy, its own dialogue and narrative. The dying scatter their clues. Just as the dead reveal the evidence of what has gone before. Sometimes.

Detective Inspector Tom Jordan picked his way over the waste ground adjacent to King's Cross Station. The surface was uneven and pitted. It was used as a car park and a place where the women working the area sometimes brought their clients. In the mornings, the place was littered with used condoms, needles and empty cans and bottles. Today was no exception.

It had rained heavily in the night. A much-needed summer downpour in the drought-ridden south-east. The early morning air was still heavy with moisture. The sun hadn't risen long enough to burn it off. Six-thirty. He'd had the call 45 minutes earlier. He'd been in bed but there had been no one else there to be disturbed.

"Thought you'd want to know, boss..."

Want! He ran a hand through his fair hair and gave the officer a look that said it all. He didn't want to know that another body had turned up on what he currently thought of as his patch. It was a fact he needed to know. A fact that he'd rather didn't exist. His stomach rumbled; lack of breakfast. He'd only had time for a coffee which he had drunk standing in the compact modern kitchen in his new-build ground floor flat, overlooking the small garden which now looked less parched but no less uncared-for. A long-awaited drenching.

Right now Tom Jordan could have done without it. Mud and bits of rubbish clung to his shoes doing nothing to improve his humour. He nodded at a couple of uniformed constables and gingerly stepped over the tape cordoning off the area where the body had been found. An ambulance was at hand, blue light flashing unnecessarily.

The photographer was just finishing the scene of crime photos as the pathologist, Josey Carhill, arrived. Black plastic covered the body. DC Doveton lifted it, his face a mask. Tom suddenly realised that the noise he had been aware of from the moment he had arrived and had ignored was WPC Avril Spenser leaning against a low brick wall and throwing up.

"Get her away from here, Doveton." His voice was a mixture of irritation and weariness. Doveton couldn't decide if the inspector was annoyed with Avril's reaction or his own inaction. He moved away smartly.

Tom bent down to stare at the inert body. It lay face to the sky as though it had been thrown there. Arms and legs akimbo. The little clothing that was left on the body – a cut-off red cotton top and miniscule skirt – was torn and now mud- and blood-spattered. Incongruously, her blond hair, darkened by the rain, gleamed in the sunlight. Bruises on her face and on every part of her body that was visible bore witness to a systematic beating. Dark brown eyes stared out of a face that looked remarkably relaxed. He could almost hear her voice. *Don't nick me now, Guv. Let me do a bit of business first.*

"Lisa." The name emerged on a breath.

The pathologist looked up, a question reflected in her eyes. She knew Tom Jordan had been brought in after the previous DI had been "retired" following "irregularities". She hoped Tom wasn't prey to them as well.

"That was her name."

"Oh." Josey closed her bag. "Well, looks like she was killed elsewhere and dumped here. Rather like the last two. There seem to be a lot of fresh needle marks on her arms. Was she a user?"

"I don't think so." Tom swore under his breath. "Time of death?"

"Anytime between nine and midnight. The rain started at about 2am and she's drenched. I'll know more when I do the post mortem."

Tom nodded mutely. He waited for the scene of crime officers to arrive and then returned to his office. He had a long day ahead of him.

TWO

Hannah Weybridge, wearing a floral-print dress she could just squeeze into under a short-sleeved linen jacket, stepped out of the taxi and searched for her purse. *Never*, she told herself for the umpteenth time, *buy a black purse and use it with a black-lined bag.* Her fingers eventually found what she was looking for and, having paid the driver, she paused at the kerbside taking in the scene she had now become a part of. Sunshine highlighted the red tones of her shoulder-length hair. Wispy curls framed her face. She donned her sunglasses and looked across the forecourt.

King's Cross was heaving. Built nearly a century and a half ago, it had a charmless air about it. The renovations, including the unprepossessing glass frontage did nothing to enhance its allure. Somehow it lacked the undercurrent of excitement that wafted through other city stations. It was not a place anyone would wish to linger. And yet the forecourt attracted – apart from the people who were there for the obvious reason – more than its share of loiterers and dawdlers.

Two young men in nondescript clothes were sitting on the ground with their backs resting against a barrier, drinking lager from cans and eyeing a group of winos who, in spite of the heat, still wore long, shapeless coats whose original colours had long since given way to drab uniformity. They seemed sexless too. The one woman among them was only distinguishable by her lack of facial hair. She laughed at something and revealed chipped and blackened teeth.

The sound drew a frown from an elegant West Indian talking into a mobile phone. His eyes were hidden behind dark glasses but his body gave the impression of a coiled spring ready for action. Regardless of the heat, he looked remarkably cool and fresh. He was standing near the kerb as a taxi pulled up almost alongside him and he jumped back smartly as the door opened.

The crowd around the various bus stops was an amorphous mess – *No nice British queues here*, Hannah thought – and, as a number 63 approached, there was a movement forward which threatened to engulf anyone in its way. A woman clutched a child in danger of being swept along. In marked contrast, the long, snaking queue for taxis was relatively sedate. Businessmen jostled with travellers laden with suitcases and subdued children, too tired from their journeys to create a fuss. A beggar was walking down the line, hat in hand, while his friend serenaded them with a penny whistle. Hannah wondered what their takings would be and looked away.

She wished she hadn't. By the station entrance a young woman sat leaning against the wall. Her face was expressionless. She looked thin and hungry as did the child who stood by her, looking eagerly at each passerby who might be encouraged to add a coin to the paltry few in the tin before them. *Some welfare state*, Hannah thought, as she walked over to them and contributed her loose change.

Feeling guilty and self-conscious, she looked at her watch. Exactly 11am, the time she had been told to meet the BBC researcher outside Casey Jones at the front of the station. And the photographer. She didn't know what he looked like either. Hannah sighed. It was one of the drawbacks about being freelance – she never seemed to work with the same photographer twice. In the five years since Hannah had given up her staff job on a woman's magazine, she'd managed with varying degrees of success to keep her career afloat. The advantages of being her own boss and not having to waste time on office politics just about outweighed the handicap of not having a regular income, paid holidays and sick leave. Having a baby, however, had caused a real blip in her finances and she was really grateful for this commission via a friend who worked on *The News* and had recommended her to the features editor of the colour supplement.

A shout rang out above the general hubbub. Hannah just caught sight of a man running across the far side of the forecourt in determined pursuit of two boys. She wondered what their crime – if any – had been or if they were actually running away from danger. No one around took any notice. No one cared. It reminded Hannah of why she was there – to interview a prostitute and a police officer who were both appearing in a documentary about the seedier side of life at King's Cross.

From the information she'd been given, the scene before her, basking in the summer sunshine, masked an underworld of vice which was low key during the day but erupted as the sun sank. Remembering the sign she'd passed recently, proclaiming that vice patrols operated in the area and offenders would be prosecuted, she glanced around curiously, wondering who were the pimps and whores, who the dope-pushers...

In the seconds that Hannah had looked away from the café and returned her gaze, a man whose profession was obvious from the cameras and paraphernalia he carried with him, had positioned himself near the entrance. Hannah braced herself – *there wouldn't be two photographers with the same rendezvous, would there?* – and approached him.

"Mike Laurel?" She smiled and held out her hand to a greyish-haired man in his mid-40s. "Hannah Weybridge."

"Hi." He had a lop-sided grin, a firm handshake and a slightly bored look about him. Hannah was immediately aware that she was of little interest to him. "Any idea what this girl looks like?" Hannah shook her head. "Well I expect she's black with a name like Princess."

That idea hadn't occurred to her. She couldn't think why the name Princess should be associated with black women. Her own daughter was already referred to that way by doting, if absentee, grandparents. The thought of Elizabeth brought a smile to her face. She could almost feel those chubby little hands clasping her neck, that beloved face smiling up at her.

She had been knocked sideways when her parents had announced they were retiring to live in France. It felt like a defection. And they didn't even speak French. Hannah had been so used to them being just an hour's drive away, it had come as an uncomfortable awakening to find them no longer within easy reach. She wrenched her mind back to the present and realised that Mike was saying something to her.

"… I only hope she isn't camera shy. These girls can be unpredictable." Hannah wondered how much Mike knew about "these girls". They were a mystery to her, a fact that did little to boost her confidence about the impending interview.

"She is being paid for her time," she pointed out, remembering the envelope of cash that had been couriered over to her the day before. "And don't hand it over until you've got the story and the photos," the features editor had warned her. "We don't want her doing a runner on us." *And don't forget to get her to sign the receipt*, Hannah added mentally.

Her gaze swept the forecourt then settled on two women walking resolutely towards them. They looked an odd pair. Height was the only thing they had in common. Raven-haired Kathy Osborne wore trousers and flat shoes and an expensive-looking designer jacket that Hannah thought she should have been able to recognise but couldn't. *Clearly worn for effect*, Hannah thought. *It's totally superfluous in this heat.* Ignoring the fact that she'd donned her own jacket to appear more professional.

Her attention passed to the other woman, no more than a girl really, who was almost a caricature of her profession: long blonde hair, minuscule skirt, black body stocking and leather waist pouch. Closer to, Hannah saw she wasn't wearing a scrap of make-up and her skin was flawless. There were slight shadows under her eyes but her instant, if hesitant, smile was engaging and made her look even younger.

They were all shaking hands and introducing themselves at the same time. Hannah thought she ought to take the initiative. "Okay, how about going for a drink and doing the interview first?" She smiled at each face trying to exude more self-assurance that she felt.

"We'll go to the Great Northern round the corner," said Kathy who, after working for months on the TV programme that the interview was to tie in with, knew the area almost as well as her companion. She had a mother hen attitude to Princess that Hannah found both irritating and a little intimidating. Princess seemed to defer to her and Hannah had no intention of conducting an interview with Kathy acting as an intermediary.

Princess and Kathy, arms linked, led the way.

THREE

Inside the bar, which had little to distinguish itself from any other hotel bar situated near a busy rail terminus, there were relatively few customers, mostly people waiting for trains and killing time. Hannah still felt self-conscious. Mike's photographic equipment and Princess's exaggerated giggles made them an obvious diversion, as everyone seemed to turn and look in their direction.

Hannah could feel the heat in her cheeks that had nothing to do with the temperature. She was as ill at ease as ever when about to ask people personal questions about their private life, especially in a public place. Never particularly confident at the interview stage, her strength lay in the writing. What she liked was to get people talking about themselves with a gentle nudge now and again. Later, she would listen to the tape several times, gradually distilling the important facts and shaping the interview to make it a good read.

Mike bought the drinks, three white wines and a pint of lager for Princess.

"You won't mind if we sit through there?" Hannah pointed to a smaller room she could see through some double glass doors. "It's quieter and I'd prefer to talk to Princess on her own."

Princess turned to the other woman as though waiting for permission. Kathy looked about to protest but mercifully didn't; she just gave the young girl's arm an encouraging squeeze before the doors separated them.

Hannah and Princess chose a table by the window and sat down. The prostitute looked relaxed, evidently enjoying all the attention. The journalist made a conscious effort to drop her shoulders and took a tape recorder out of her bag.

"Don't don't worry about this." She smiled at the girl, forgetting completely that she'd already been filmed and recorded. "I can concentrate on you and not worry about taking notes. Just say something so I can check the voice level."

Princess giggled. "Testing… testing… 1, 2, 3," she said in what she thought of as a posh voice. Then her expression and tone changed; it sounded more gravelly. "Look, have you got the money?"

"Yes, I…" *Help*, thought Hannah. *Please don't ask for it now before we've even started the interview.*

"In cash? I haven't got a bank account."

"Yes, don't worry. I…"

"I want more," Princess interrupted her again. "My story's got to be worth more than a measly 100 quid."

Although she didn't say so, Hannah couldn't help agreeing with her. Her last commission had been to interview a man cleared of a rape charge; he'd been paid £1000 for his side of a story, which had already appeared in all the tabloids. Here the girl was going to expose herself for one tenth of that. It wasn't fair but Hannah hadn't negotiated the sum. For a moment, she wondered who had. *Kathy? Then, why so low?*

"I'm sorry," she said. "I'm not staff so I really don't have any influence at the paper." She hoped she sounded convincing. She herself was desperate for her own fee and didn't fancy losing the interview.

Princess took a long gulp of lager, lit a cigarette and eyed the journalist through the smoke she exhaled. Her expression was unreadable. Hannah thought she was going to make more of a protest and wondered how to deal with it. She was wrong.

"Well see if you can…" Princess's voice trailed off. For a second she looked so young and vulnerable. It hit Hannah in that moment that she was just about old enough to be the girl's mother. It was an odd but not original thought. Ageing didn't worry Hannah and maternity in her mid-30s had brought a dimension to her life that was both surprising and fulfilling. It made her wonder now, with heightened awareness, how any woman – whatever her circumstances – could let this happen to her child.

"How old are you, Princess?"

The girl blew a smoke ring and seemed pleased with the achievement. "19. Do you think I look 19? I always looked old for my age." She spoke quickly, excitedly, like a child.

Hannah smiled, at the moment Princess looked about 16. "How long have you been working?"

"Five or six years, I suppose. Look I've written it all down. When I knew I was going talk to you, I started writing it all down. I usually try to forget. I don't know what it's going to do to me. Bringing it all up."

Hannah glanced at the three red exercise books Princess had produced, filled with childlike script and felt humbled. She sipped her wine. "Why don't you just tell me what happened, in your own words." She smiled, intrigued by the girl's accent which was a curious mixture of nasal North London vowels, lazy consonants and something altogether more refined. She also wondered how important Princess's role had been in the documentary. Maybe they hadn't asked her too many questions.

Princess consulted the notebooks and read in a monotone voice: "I was ten when my parents broke up. Mum was left to bring up the three of us – me and my two younger sisters – and we never had much money. My granddad died then as well and I started bunking school and spending more and more time on the streets. My mum shacked up with another man. He was always trying to have it off with me and in the end, he raped me." The horror of it was at variance with her matter-of-fact tone.

"Wasn't your mother aware of what was going on?" Hannah was appalled and gulped some more wine.

Princess shrugged. "It's not the sort of thing you can talk to your mother about, is it?"

Hannah fervently hoped that she'd be the type of mother her daughter would be able to talk to about anything. Then she remembered her own mother's reaction when she told her she was pregnant.

Daphne Weybridge had been incredulous. "But darling, how could you? In this day and age?"

"These things happen," said Hannah. "Contraception does fail."

Her mother's face wore an odd expression – awkward. "And what does Paul have to say about it?" Daphne had never had a high opinion of the man she assumed would eventually be a son-in-law.

For a moment Hannah thought about the truth then decided to modify it for her mother. "Paul isn't around anymore and wants no contact with the child."

Daphne had given Hannah one of her looks. It was obvious she wanted to say a great deal but settled on, "Well I never thought it would happen to the daughter of mine." Her face was puce with indignation.

"Look, Mother, I'm 34 not a 16-year-old. I've got my own home and a career and now I'm going to have a baby – on my own."

"Well, I wish you luck," said Daphne. "I don't know what your father will have to say."

As it happened, her father – to Daphne's fury – was delighted for her. But his support was short-lived. Rather sheepishly, the man who had worked for an insurance company all his life and had never been interested in foreign holidays, told her of their migration to the Loire Valley. Hannah was astonished. She couldn't help thinking that her mother had engineered their retirement to coincide with her own maternity. They had, however, been around for the birth and were delighted with their grandchild, if not with their only daughter.

Hannah sighed at the memory. She, for all her maturity, had been unable to convince her mother that she was doing the right thing. How could a pubescent girl succeed with a mother weighed down by financial insecurity, who was determined to see no ill in her new man?

"But me mum was worried about me," Princess assured her, "and eventually she went to the welfare people." The girl paused for a gulp of lager and another cigarette. "They did do one of those 28-day place of safety order things. When she tried to get me back, they did it again, didn't they? And again until finally I was taken into care for good."

"How did you feel about that?"

Princess wound a strand of hair around a finger, then inspected it for split ends. An absorbing activity.

"Surely it was better than living with a man who raped you?" Hannah prompted.

"You mus' be joking." The girl's laugh held no humour. "The staff were having sex with each other and with the kids. They were taking us on holiday, letting us get drunk, do what we liked, when we really needed to be taught to be good. Kids were even sniffing glue on the premises and I had a go at it."

She paused, as if waiting for a comment, but Hannah only nodded. She wasn't sure how much of this she believed but she didn't want to interrupt the flow.

"In the end, I ran away," the girl continued. "I came here an' met up with this woman. Linda her name was." Princess's voice trembled becoming almost a whisper. "I didn't know she ran a brothel. I didn't even know what a brothel was, but I needed some money and…" Momentarily, her composure cracked and Hannah saw an even younger face contorted with the pain the memories evoked.

The penniless young girl's fate had been sealed. Princess had never really stood a chance. Linda, she learned, had some unsavoury friends and Princess suddenly found herself at the mercy of two heavies.

"If I didn't have the money at the end of the day, they used to get hold of a big clump of wood and spank me with it, fuckin' hard." The girl's voice seemed suddenly loud.

Hannah glanced over at the elderly couple a few tables away. They were patently getting some vicarious pleasure from listening to this poor girl's story but no more so than the tabloid buyers destined to read Hannah's article. The woman in her felt sick. The journalist nodded.

"I'm not joking," the gravelly voice went on. "If I didn't have that money, I was in fuckin' trouble. And I didn't even know how to do it, never mind anything else." Princess managed a smile. "I'd get in a car and if they said how much, I'd say well how much do you think I should get?"

Princess gulped her lager and stubbed out her cigarette, lighting another one immediately. She didn't want to remember the shit she'd gone through. The smell of stale breath, sweat and semen; the pain that her body endured time and again and the awful things men, who one minute looked and sounded so nice, mouthed into her ear as they abused her and then almost threw her out of the car when they had finished with her – sometimes without even paying. She shook her head to try and stop more memories surfacing in her mind.

FOUR

"Not much to show for her life, is it?" DI Tom Jordan was inspecting some of the bagged-up belongings from Lisa's flat. There were no surprises. Her landlady hadn't seen her for two weeks, as Spenser and Doveton discovered when they visited the address they had for Lisa.

"But she was often not around for a while. One of the reasons I liked having her here." Shirley Lane, leaning heavily on a walking stick, had let them into the flat without asking to see the warrant.

"So there was no reason to report her missing?" WPC Spenser, recovered from her bout of vomiting earlier that day, was writing in her notebook.

Shirley, who could have been any age between late 40s and early 60s, wiped an imaginary speck of dust from the table they were sitting at. She was smartly turned out in a neat cotton frock, almost as though she were expecting visitors. "Like I said, she was often out – overnight, a few days."

"What did she do?" Pen poised, Avril feigned disinterest. "For a living?"

"Oh, I'm not sure really – something to do with PR and seeing clients?"

It was all Avril could do to stop herself snorting. "You didn't ask for references when she moved in?"

"No." Shirley tucked a wisp of light brown hair behind her ear. "Wasn't necessary. She gave me a large deposit – in cash. She seemed a very private person and so am I, Officer."

Avril made a point of reading through her notes as DS Doveton came back into the sitting room.

"Thank you, Mrs Lane – "

"Miss."

"Thank you, Miss Lane. You've been very helpful. And you say Lisa didn't have any friends phone or drop in?" The woman shook her head.

Blood from the proverbial stone, thought Doveton, but he managed to smile. "All Lisa's possessions are being removed and we'll just need to take your fingerprints to eliminate them."

"Won't she be coming back, then?" Shirley Lane asked as each finger was pressed into the inkpad and then recorded. There was something in the way she asked this that made Avril look up, but the grey eyes which met hers gave nothing away.

A look passed between the officers. "No, Miss Lane, her family have asked us to remove everything."

"But, I …"

"If you have any further questions, or have any ideas about Lisa's whereabouts, Miss Lane, please ring this number." Doveton handed her a card. It stuck in his throat that he had to lie. That he couldn't tell this woman the reason Lisa wouldn't be coming back was that she was, at this moment, on a slab in the mortuary.

Just before they left, Avril asked to use the bathroom.

"Just through there." Shirley pointed her in the right direction.

If Avril thought there would be something of interest, she was disappointed. Lisa obviously kept all her toiletries in her room. Then, just as she flushed the loo, she noticed a box tucked away on a shelf behind some towels. A huge box of condoms. Miss Lane's or Lisa's? Whoever they belonged to, Shirley Lane must have known they were there. It threw an altogether different light on their relationship.

Doveton was saying something about the weather when Avril emerged and they took their leave.

Within ten minutes, they were back at the station and writing up their reports. Miss Lane obviously wanted to know more, but they'd kept her out of the way when the scene of crime team broke the lock on the wardrobe, the contents of which revealed Lisa's trade. Hardly the clothes and accessories for a PR. Photographs were taken of everything in situ before they were bagged up.

DI Jordan was looking at those photos now.

"Someone's daughter, sister, friend and no one has missed her."

"Well, it's hardly going to be front page news." Doveton's tone betrayed his sense of frustration. His new boss was an enigma. They all knew why DI Thornton had taken "medical" retirement and some had more to fear from the new broom than others.

Tom's face was unreadable. "Let me know when the PM report comes through. I'm going home to change."

FIVE

Princess glanced at the journalist's face through a haze of smoke: a picture of self-righteous middle-class concern. *She doesn't have a fucking clue,* she thought, then continued her story. "Luckily, luckily I met a community worker from Brixton. He used to work in legal aid or housing or something and he was a friend of Linda's, right, but straight. Now, he helped me a lot."

"What's his name?"

Princess hesitated. "Tony. Tony Vitello," she said quietly. "But you won't put his name in the paper, will you?"

"Not if you don't want me to. I can leave his name out."

The girl looked relieved. "He wouldn't like it, would he." It was not a question.

"And what did he want from you?" Hannah didn't believe in knights in shining armour.

"Nothing. He wasn't into sex. He was really good at that kung fu stuff. He beat up these two guys when they were threatening me with a hatchet." Hannah's eyes widened. "I was shit scared, I can tell you. But he was great..." Princess's face lit up momentarily.

Then, her mood changed again. "Afterwards," she said brusquely, "he arranged for me to stay with a social worker he knew. Gaynor, her name was. I didn't know she was lesbian," said Princess flatly.

Some luck, thought Hannah wryly. *How can anyone have so many cards stacked against them?* "Did he know that?"

"What?" Princess, a train of thought broken, looked at her vacantly.

"Your community worker, Tony, did he know about the social worker?"

Princess shook her head. "I don't know." She looked as though the thought had never crossed her mind. There was a second or so when Hannah thought she'd made some connection, but the moment was lost. Princess took up the narrative as though the interruption had not occurred.

"She got short of cash and had to go hustling for big money – people who wanted lesbian scenes."

Hannah almost choked on her wine. "Why?"

"Why what?"

"Why did she have to go hustling, as you put it? Why didn't she just borrow from the bank?"

Princess looked blank. "I don't know. I suppose I didn't ask her. I just did as I was told."

"Was she already on the game then?" Hannah persisted.

"I don't know! Look, all I know is that she went for people who wanted lesbian scenes, right?" Her tone was belligerent, hostile.

"I'm sorry," Hannah murmured and touched the girl's hand lightly. "Go on."

Princess consulted her notebook, sighed theatrically and cleared her throat.

"Please go on," the journalist prompted.

The girl continued as she lit another cigarette. "They'd phone you up and ask you to dress up for them and come round. Imagine big red lips and high heels and going out like a bloody tart!"

Hannah smiled. The irony was clearly lost on Princess.

"We used to get about £600 a night."

"How much?" Hannah thought she must have misheard the amount.

"600 quid," Princess said with more than a hint of pride in her voice.

"But what happened to all that money? Your share?"

Princess pursed her lips. "Dunno. Gaynor kept it, I suppose. She gave me pocket money though and she didn't charge me any keep to stay with her."

I should hope not! thought Hannah. "What happened then?" she asked, still reeling from the amount of money Princess and Gaynor had earned.

"She started getting jealous, didn't she?" Princess pulled a face. "She was a bloody nymphomaniac – all she wanted to do was keep having it off with me all the time, but I didn't want that and I moved out."

"Did your friend help you?" Hannah wondered what else could go wrong. "Did Tony help you?"

"No, he wasn't around then." Princess toyed with the almost empty glass. Hannah managed to catch Mike's eye through the glass door and signalled for refills.

"I found a room and started working the beat on the Edgware Road and King's Cross. I did it because I needed the money and it's all I knew how to do. All I've been taught." She drained her glass. "We're like a family here. It's my home."

Hannah felt a deep sadness. She didn't want to believe what she was hearing. A 14-year-old girl abused mentally and physically by just about everyone she came into contact with. Her "family", a network of whores, drug addicts and down-and-outs who provided her education. Her "home", the car parks and disused and derelict buildings around the station where she plied her trade.

"What about your family? Do you see your mother or father?"

"My dad was in the army. So we didn't see him much. He was a sergeant major." Hannah doubted that, but the girl's eyes lit up with pride. "It was my mum's fault they broke up – stupid cow couldn't keep her knickers on."

Princess stared into the bottom of her glass. "He got married again and moved away up North. I did go and see him once, but I just couldn't tell him what was happening. He used to call me his little princess. I didn't want him to know what I become."

The girl sniffed loudly.

"And your mother?" Hannah prompted.

"She couldn't help. She didn't have any money and she's got two more kids now. She's still with the same man… I send them money, you know for my sisters, when I can. I keep hoping she'll get rid of him…"

The click of the cassette recorder interrupted them. Hannah turned the tape over. She felt numbed, humbled. She had the feeling she was going to hear worse.

Mike came through the door and brought over more drinks. He glanced at the two women's faces, said nothing and walked away. Through the glass door, Hannah could see him talking to Kathy. She wondered how the researcher who had spent so much time with these women had coped. Had she managed to preserve her professional objectivity? How could she not feel in some way contaminated by this world where sex is just a commodity and casual violence a way of life?

"Have you ever been attacked?"

"You're joking?" Princess rolled back her left sleeve to reveal a jagged, healed scar running almost the length of her forearm.

"How on earth –?"

"A punter who didn't want to pay." The resignation in Princess's voice was heartbreaking. "I'm always being fucking done over or threatened. It goes with the job. One night I got a chauffeur and went to an NCP car park I used. I thought there was something funny. He was wearing these black gloves. He bent forward – to give me the money, I'm thinking – and he came out with a corkscrew knife. I shit myself. I got out of the car and ran over to the attendant who I'm paying to look after me and he just locks the door and hides under the table. So I ran up this little alleyway to a block of flats where there's a porter and he said I could stay there until the guy goes. I couldn't go out for ages after that even though I was broke."

"But you do keep working on the streets?"

"Yeah." Princess gazed out of the window, then turned her attention back to her interviewer. "It's even more dangerous now, you know. You get into a car and you don't know who you're fucking getting in with because the old Bill are so hot, right, looking out for you all the time. I've been nicked loads of times. But really, if the punters weren't hanging around, there'd be no one there to do it with, would there?"

Her expression appeared to be an attempt at a wide-eyed innocence. It didn't quite come off. "I've lived in this area all my working life. Why should I move out? It's them who ask me."

"What sort of men are they?

Princess gulped her drink then leaned forward confidentially. "All sorts. Some of them are real perverts. It makes me sick. They ask if I can get them an eight-year-old then get off by telling me what they would like to do with her. They ought to be fucking locked away. Some of them are quite nice but they're so thick." She rolled her eyes to the ceiling. "They ask 'what do you like doing?' They don't realise we don't want to enjoy it at all. I lay down with them and pretend, but I don't feel a thing. I've never come in my life."

There was a moment's silence as Hannah collected her thoughts. Her own experience of sex was so different. She thought about Paul and the pleasure his body had given her on and off for five years – before her pregnancy. Would he ever have gone with a prostitute? Would her father? Or any of her male friends? She liked to think not, but what did she know. Some of the men who had paid Princess must have had wives or girlfriends or indeed daughters her age. It made her shudder just to think about the possibilities and consequences.

"What about Aids? VD?"

"I always, always have regular health checks and I always use condoms." Princess's assurance came out like a set piece, parrot fashion, said for the journalist's benefit. Hannah was not convinced and wondered if Kathy had briefed her on what to say. She was even more sceptical when the girl told her she had a few regulars who took her for "slap-up meals" and to posh hotels. Then she thought, *Why not?*

"I won't kiss the punters and I don't always do sex with them. I do a 'play around'."

"What's that?"

Princess's expression spoke volumes. Hannah obviously didn't rate highly in her eyes. "A lot of them like to sit in the car and play with themselves, right, or he plays with himself and you play with yourself. You wear stockings and suspenders and talk some disgusting things about 13, 14, eight-year-olds. If I didn't do this, they would do it to them. One guy said that to me the other night…

Of course if you are willing to do more, you get paid more."

"And how much do you get paid?"

Princess looked coy. "Depends what you do." She took a gulp of lager, and removed another cigarette but didn't light it. "Loads of punters want to do it up your arse. But I won't do that. Most girls won't."

In spite of her language and what she was talking about, Princess had a curious air of naivety about her. It was hard to believe that she worked, as she claimed, from nine o'clock in the evening until the early hours of the morning, night in, night out.

"I just blank it all out. If I don't blank it out, I'll just crack up," she said dully. "I just want to get out of it and live a normal life. Get married, have babies. You got any children?"

"Just one. She's six months old."

"I wouldn't work if I had a baby," Princess said, almost dreamily.

"I don't have a choice." It was only after she had declared this, somewhat defensively, that Hannah realised what Princess had meant by work. Her own option was a darn sight easier.

"What's her name?"

"Elizabeth. I…" Hannah felt some details of her own life were a fair deal, a trade-off, but she didn't want to get too personal.

Princess went dewy-eyed. "D'you know when I see people walking along the street, getting up in the morning to go to work, having families, I feel really jealous. I want to get out of it while I'm still young." The girl's voice had lost its gravelly edge.

She looked so lost… So… Hannah didn't want to think about it.

"That's great, Princess." Hannah switched off the tape recorder, taking her time to put it in her bag so that she wouldn't have to look into those eyes. She wanted to say something more but she couldn't find the right words. Everything seemed so trite in face of the girl's tragedy.

"My name is Caroline."

"I'm sorry?"

"My real name is Caroline. But don't use it in the article, will you?"

"No, of course not." Hannah paused. Honesty made her add, "People will recognise you, you know. What about your parents?"

"I shouldn't think they'll read it. I don't suppose they even know what I look like now."

◊ ◊ ◊

Hannah and Kathy trailed behind Mike and Princess. It was embarrassing to witness. Princess was really playing her part. She had put on far too much make-up and arranged her hair differently. She looked every inch a hooker and posed outrageously to Mike's enthusiastic directions. Hannah wondered about the appropriateness of some of the shots and it crossed her mind he might be intending to use some of the photos for other outlets. *Ripped off again, Princess,* she thought.

"Do you do a lot of these interviews?" Kathy asked

Hannah hesitated. "I do a lot of human interest articles. But I've never interviewed a prostitute before. I found it harrowing to say the least."

"Yes." Kathy's gaze trailed Princess's performance. "I hadn't a clue about this area before researching for the programme. Three months here is enough, believe me."

And Princess? Hannah wanted to ask but was interrupted by Mike's shout of "Great, just lean back a fraction". Then he was packing away his cameras.

It was over. Hannah got Princess to sign a receipt and handed over the money in the envelope.

"Come and have a drink?" Princess invited Kathy and the two women linked arms and walked away. Hannah was curious about their relationship. Was Kathy genuinely fond of her or was the apparent friendship just a means to an end? How would the younger girl feel when the researcher moved on to her next assignment, as she was about to do? Betrayed again? Princess was being used by everyone – including her and Mike. She was a walking victim.

"Bit of a lost cause, isn't she?" Mike commented as they snatched a quick sandwich lunch before their next interview, again at the Great Northern. "I gave her an extra tenner."

"Did you? That was kind." Hannah's suspicions confirmed, she felt uncomfortable in the knowledge that she could probably prove nothing. And who would care anyway?

SIX

The inspector confounded Hannah's idea of a police officer. Though to be fair most of her impressions were drawn from TV cops… She hadn't known what to expect but he was altogether too… too… Hannah couldn't put her finger on what was unsettling her.

Tom Jordan was tall with an athletic build, good-looking in an offbeat sort of way, and eyes a penetrating a blue with a darker circle around the iris. He looked about 38 and was, as they say, at ease in his own body. Mike and Hannah glanced at each other and smiled.

Hannah felt this interview was going to be more relaxed and so Mike was going to sit in on it. He poured Tom a coffee as the policeman explained he'd begun working for the police eight years ago after becoming disillusioned with teaching and he hadn't regretted his career change.

It seemed an amazing redirection to Hannah. "You must have had to harden yourself up," she commented.

"Oh, the Force did that for me. It makes you much more cynical and resilient but not uncaring." He sipped his coffee and Hannah noticed the rather unusual signet ring on his right hand. The tape recorder was switched on and she was doodling on her pad, unconsciously reproducing the ring's curious insignia. It looked like two letters intertwined, but she couldn't make out which they were.

"I think a lot of police officers are very caring people," DI Jordan said as if in reply to an unspoken question from Hannah.

He sounds like a publicity handout, she thought.

"Initially I was a bit naive and I suppose my political views changed quite a bit. I used to be left wing and now I'm more conservative – with a small c," he added.

Of course! Hannah groaned inwardly; this was not the type of police officer she'd either expected or – if she were honest – wanted. His views wouldn't make particularly inspiring copy. Some right-wing attitudes would have been more typical, she felt, but had to concede that he'd look good in the photographs.

"So how do you come to be at King's Cross?"

"I was –" there was the briefest of pauses – "promoted seven months ago. As soon as I got here, I was aware there was an enormous problem. King's Cross seems to attract the lowlife of London: vagrants, winos, beggars, prostitutes, drug dealers and users. They all flock to the forecourt. I was horrified. It was shocking, not the kind of place you'd want your wife or girlfriend come and wait for you."

Hannah wondered idly about his wife or girlfriend. Or both, she thought. He was an attractive man. Rather like Paul.

"So," Tom Jordan continued, "we decided to make a concerted effort to clear the forecourt and the surrounding area, our little patch of London."

Hannah coughed. "This was to be your initiative?"

Tom interlaced his fingers and studied his palms, lips pursed.

"Mostly mine," he agreed. "We took officers from uniform and put them into plainclothes and put them on permanent lates, just to go out on the front of the station to see what was happening and if they saw people involved with drugs and prostitution to arrest and charge them. By making it harder for them, we're clearing the area. I think it's working," said Tom, smiling at Hannah.

"But won't the prostitutes just go elsewhere?"

"Of course." Tom spread his hands. The nails looked as though he'd recently had a manicure. It was an odd thought to cross her mind. "It's a social problem, not a police problem. There used to be as many as 80 prostitutes working the forecourt; that number has been reduced to about 20 or 30. I think I know most of them."

Hannah looked up from her pad. "Do you know a girl who calls herself Princess?"

There was an almost imperceptible pause. Tom hadn't known which prostitute had been chosen for the interview. *Thank God it hadn't been...* A flicker of an eyelid betrayed a slight unease. "Yes. Sad case that." He held Hannah's gaze. "We do try to get them to see social welfare workers, but we can't make them. A lot of them actually want to be on the game. They don't want any do-gooders trying to reform them."

"I suppose not." Hannah tried a different tack. "How well do you get to know these women?"

"Quite well really," said Tom, deliberately ignoring the implication of Hannah's question. "There's a fairly friendly relationship between us." Hannah had her doubts about that. "They regard being picked up three or four times a week as an occupational hazard. I regard it as their way of paying their taxes." Tom laughed.

God how pompous! Hannah thought but smiled.

Tom Jordan eyed her over the rim of his coffee cup. Disapproval was written all over her face. It was rather refreshing really.

"It's a unique relationship actually. They're a little bit peeved when they're arrested, as you'd expect. The reason they get annoyed is that it takes them off the streets for an hour or two and they don't earn the money.

"At Clerkenwell, the court they go to, they get fined £20 to £25, less than one punter. Some of them are earning phenomenal amounts of money. You can pull them with £300 or £400 on them, which they would have earned that night."

"As much as that?" Mike looked as though he was having second thoughts about giving Princess some extra money.

"Well that's the real pros. There's a definite pecking order among the women. Some of them get furious when the younger ones undercut them."

"Why would they do that? Surely it's in their interest to make as much money as possible." Hannah met his gaze.

"You'd think so wouldn't you? The more professional ones are much better at negotiating and they have a definite business plan, saving for a mortgage, kids' schools…" He noticed Hannah's raised eyebrow. "Some of them send their kids to very good boarding schools, you know. However, some of the younger ones just want enough money for their next fix."

Hannah wondered where Princess fitted in this social pecking order. "So they are arrested…?"

"Yes and it is the time off the street they resent. Although from the time a prostitute's arrested to the time she's bailed can be less than an hour, a couple of hours at most." Tom Jordan held her gaze and grinned. "She can be back at King's Cross station before we are."

"Isn't that all rather futile?"

Tom smiled his easy smile. He was a very effective PR man.

"Well, that depends on your point of view, doesn't it? I think there's a mutual respect between us. When we pull them in, we often get information on other rackets. And if there's ever an incident involving a child, you can guarantee the prostitutes will pull out all the stops for us. And, just as importantly, they feel able to report crimes against them. We've had a few incidents when a prostitute has been raped and they reported it; they're not scared to."

Hannah's mind went to Princess's injured arm; she hadn't mentioned reporting it to the police.

"One or two of the local prostitutes have had ribs broken, faces slashed by punters and we tried the best we can to get who's done it." Tom paused, pensive. "It's a dangerous game. If they get into a car with someone, the next 20 minutes or so is out of their hands, whereas when they go to a place around the station they are more in control of the situation because they know the area and the punter might not."

"You evidently know the area too. How did you feel the first time you caught someone in the act?"

"A bit awkward but now I can laugh about it. The girls don't get embarrassed even though they might pretend to be. The most embarrassed is definitely the punter who can't wait to get away. And I waste no sympathy on them. I don't have any respect for the blokes who go with prostitutes, no respect at all," he declared.

Does he protest too much? Hannah wondered briefly. "What about the women?" she asked. "How do you relate to them?"

"A lot of the prostitutes I talk to I quite like. They're honest and have a very earthy sense of humour. Sometimes they are hilarious. And some of them you think how could anyone go with that, but they get punters even though they are so horrendous."

"Do they ever proposition you?" Hannah asked.

Tom laughed again. "One or two have tried. But it's not on, is it? I know prostitutes claim that police demand sexual favours in exchange for not being arrested, but I don't think it really happens – not very often anyway." He held Hannah's gaze. His blue eyes were having a mesmeric effect on her. To distract herself, she poured some coffee.

"Of course," DI Jordan continued, "they do get to recognise us but it doesn't put them off being friendly, greeting you when you see them. We get one that causes an absolute scene, shouting and screaming when you arrest her, but if you see her out of that situation, she's as nice as pie.

"There's a girl called Lisa and if you bump into her, she says…" Tom's voice petered out. Hannah was convinced he had paled a little under his light tan.

Mike coughed into the silence; he was clearly bored.

"She says…" Hannah prompted.

Tom collected his thoughts. "She says, don't nick me now, nick me in an hour. Let me do a bit of business first. And if you go back in an hour, she'll get into the van without saying a word."

Hannah must have looked disbelieving.

"It's not a crusade you know. We're not here to persecute them. Whether you arrest 10 or 20, the problem is still there, so you might as well do it with a smile and a bit of compassion. If you leave them for ten minutes, is the world going to be a worse place?"

He sounds too good to be true, thought Hannah. *I wonder if he really believes all this.* She switched off the tape. "Thanks Tom. Have you got a number I can contact you at if I need to clarify anything?"

Tom handed her an embossed card with both his office and home numbers. His fingers brushed her palm and a tingle of anticipation seemed to pass between them. In spite of the heat, a cold tremor ran the length of her body.

"Right well, let's go and get some shots shall we?" Mike suggested.

They all stood up. "You don't need me for this, so I'll leave you to it." Hannah smiled at both men and shook hands. A shaft of sunlight caught Tom's ring. It gave her an uneasy feeling, although for the life of her, she couldn't have explained why.

Within minutes of leaving the men, her mind was far away. The seediness of King's Cross faded as she sat back in a taxi, sighed and slipped off her sandals. Her mind was filled with her child and she ached to kiss her plump cheeks and hear Elizabeth's delighted gurgles when she returned home. But unbidden came the image of Princess…

SEVEN

The police tape had gone – all but a small piece that clung to an upturned crate. Nothing was left to show of the drama that had been played out earlier that morning. Even the mud had dried. The rubbish that littered the area, however, remained.

Detective Inspector Jordan almost enjoyed walking around the station's environs and pointing out the prostitutes' favourite haunts to Mike Laurel. A disused car, a bricked-in doorway, an alleyway, the space between two parked cars – anywhere out of direct light and view would do for the hooker and, presumably, client alike.

From what he understood from research studies on the subject, and he had been doing a lot of reading up on prostitution, fear of detection was, for some men, all part of the excitement of going with whores. The reason for it, in some cases. He had ceased to be surprised by the cross-section of male society that found its way to the area, but it still made him feel uncomfortable. And catching women with their skirts up and men with their pants down was not what he joined the Force for.

The photographer was easy to work with. Tom had felt self-conscious at first, but as Mike clicked away, he had relaxed. The journalist, on the other hand, was a different matter. Hannah Weybridge had unsettled him. She wasn't what he'd expected. His image of female tabloid journalists was of hard-bitten hacks door-stepping the homes of victims of tragedies and scandals. Seducing friends and relations with the wave of a fat cheque. Hannah certainly didn't fit that stereotype; she was rounded on the edges and he found himself feeling strangely protective of her. He was glad she hadn't accompanied them for the photographs. The area was all so sordid with used condoms and needles adding to the other debris.

Thinking of Hannah, he smiled to himself and rather hoped she would need to ring him. The article, at any rate, would be good PR. He'd been happy with what he'd seen in a preview of the documentary – the Force was definitely shown in a sympathetic, user-friendly way. The newspaper feature would reinforce the image and the powers-that-be would be pleased.

As he walked through the open plan offices to his own partitioned-off area, WPC Avril Spenser called out, "How did it go, Sir?"

Tom smiled. "No problem."

He repeated the same thought to the sergeant who came into his office a few moments later.

"No awkward questions, then?" Brian Jones asked.

"No, Jones, the news blackout has been effective and this was a soft touch. Women's magazine stuff." He sighed and looked at the file Brian Jones had placed before him. "No leads at all on this one?"

"No and it's not the usual sort of pimp's revenge either. It just doesn't make sense."

"Does murder ever make sense, Jones?" It was a rhetorical question but one it looked as though Jones was going to try and answer. Tom diverted him as he looked down at the scene of crime photos. "Alas poor Lisa," he said, gently, "that you should amount to this."

Jones coughed. "You don't think there's something more to this, sir?"

"In what way, sergeant?" Tom looked up, enquiringly.

"I don't know. It's just a feeling I get when I'm talking to the other women. It's as though they know something but are too scared to talk."

"Go on."

"Well, I get the feeling that there's some sort of group – organisation – behind all this."

"There are plenty of organised rackets around here."

"No, something more upmarket." Tom raised an eyebrow at Jones' choice of words. "Some sort of influential group of men, you know like the…"

"Yes, Jones," Tom cut him off. "I follow your meaning." He closed the file abruptly, angry with both himself and Jones. This was the third dead prostitute on his manor and the feeling in his bones was that she wouldn't be the last. But there was nothing to connect the three murders – yet. The irony was that he'd been brought in to clean up the area after the previous inspector been linked to various vice rackets and had been given medical retirement.

Tom sighed and forced himself to smile, albeit wearily, at Jones. Now the unthinkable had happened. Things had actually got worse. "How about chasing up that post mortem report?" He twisted the ring on his finger absent-mindedly.

EIGHT

Hannah was sitting at a desk in her study, which would have been the third bedroom in her turn-of-the-century terraced house. It had been her home now just over seven years and the rooms had evolved around her. Framed theatre programmes clustered on the walls in the hall. In every room, shelves bowed under the weight of books. Furniture had been collected by inspiration rather than design, so that a rosewood dresser in the dining-room was mate to a more modern gate-leg table that had been donated by an uncle.

Edwardian knick-knacks received from her grandparents' home and old, lovingly restored family photographs in ancient frames gave a sense of period to the dining and sitting rooms. Only the kitchen was really modern, gleaming white against a pale blue. Hannah liked to sit at the circular table with the book propped up against something as she ate a solitary breakfast – that is if she didn't take a coffee at into the tiny garden that was so peaceful in the early morning. The high fences and trees from neighbouring gardens blocked noise, so that you'd hardly believe you were in the middle of a city.

The study overlooked the garden and Hannah sat at right angles to the window so she could turn and stare out whenever inspiration failed her. Now, however, she smiled at the photographs of Elizabeth arranged ad hoc on the wall in front of her.

Until the birth of her daughter, Hannah had lived alone. Now sharing her home even with her own child, took some getting used to – the plastic ducks and all the paraphernalia in the bathroom, toys all over the house. Hannah wondered what it would be like as Elizabeth grew older and acquired more and more possessions… The thought made her feel guilty. Families of four or more lived quite happily in these houses. The house next door was home to a family of five.

Hannah had been happy with her own company. Paul had only ever been an occasional weekend guest. They both liked their own space too much to consider sharing. At least that was what Hannah had thought. Her pregnancy had thrown new light on their relationship. Paul did want to marry one day, he said, but he didn't want to tie himself to Hannah or her baby.

"Are you sure it's mine?" he asked, his eyes unable to meet hers.

She shouldn't have been shocked that Paul should come out with such an old line but she was. Her expression would have doused a blazing fire. He had the grace to apologise. But there was a sting.

"I'm sorry, but it's me or the baby. I just don't want to be a father – yet."

It was the "yet" which hurt her most of all. Such a small word but a huge betrayal. Paul had taken her hand and stroked her palm. "You can still have me if…" He let the "if" hang in the air and his tone assumed Hannah's compliance. Another betrayal. He was stunned when she asked him to leave. She hadn't seen him since and yet, sometimes, when she looked into her daughter's face, her father's expression seemed to mock her…

The ringing of the phone broke into her reveries. Hannah always allowed it three rings before answering. It had become a ritual with her. Like counting the stairs as she went up them. It was, of course, reassuringly the same number every time.

"Hello, Hannah Weybridge."

"Han – nah hi. Stewart Granger here. Great piece on the prostitute."

"Thank you." Hannah held her breath, fingers crossed.

"We just need a bit more detail about what she actually does." Stewart stretched out each syllable to give it maximum impact. "You know the sort of thing."

Hannah's heart sank. She hated having to fiddle with a piece once it was written and she had hoped Stewart's call meant another commission. "But I thought *The News* was supposed to be a family newspaper?"

"It is, it is. We just want you to put everything in and we'll go through with the blue pencil this end." His voice sounded even smarmier if that were possible.

Hannah couldn't see the point but she needed the money and couldn't afford to upset anyone. "Fine. When do you want it by?"

"Soon as. You know everything needed yesterday."

"I'll fax it over to you this afternoon."

"Great stuff. It's scheduled for Thursday week to tie in with the programme in the evening. Pics are super by the way."

"Oh good." They would be wouldn't they? "I'll ring you this afternoon when the copy's ready."

"Great. Bye."

NINE

Princess was lying on top of her bed, writing in one of her red notebooks. She glanced at her watch. Five o'clock – plenty of time before she had to leave. She cupped her chin in her hand and paused for thought. So much was going round in her mind.

The bed doubled as a sofa in the small room that comprised her home. A previous tenant had curtained off the kitchen alcove, hiding the stainless steel sink and the motley collection of pots and pans that she rarely used. There was a small fridge and a little spin dryer which she'd bought herself to save on visits to the launderette. And the other door in the room led to a tiny loo and shower room.

The walls were covered with photographs meticulously cut out from glossy magazines. Princess Di vied for position with a still from *The Bodyguard* and another from *Sister Act*. She loved the cinema. Sometimes she went to matinées with some of the girls, usually Lisa and Mimi. The photographs displayed a luxurious lifestyle that was in marked contrast to where they hung. Peeling paintwork, faded wallpaper, yellowed from a series of inhabitants' smoking and a threadbare rug was hardly designer living. She'd only been here two weeks and hadn't got round to smartening the place up.

She'd had to leave the last flat rather quickly when the landlord discovered how she earned his rent and decided he'd like more of a cut. When Princess refused, he produced a knife and held it against her throat, promising a new look for her face if she didn't comply next time he asked for a percentage.

And he had someone watching the house. A few days later, Princess had left the building carrying the pink bag she often took out with her to work, only this time it was packed to capacity with her clothes, cosmetics and most treasured possession – a leather-bound frame of a young man in an army uniform. It now held pride of place on the wall.

She had found the bedsit through Sam at the station's lost property office. Princess and the other working girls often left things with him if they needed to during the day and he was always ready with a mug of tea and some gossip. He was the eyes and ears of the Cross; a sad character who always appeared chirpy. Most of the girls adored him and he was never charged for his "relief".

Now he was her neighbour in the next room and had offered to help decorate. Princess dreamed of the tastefully furnished hotel rooms and luxurious bathrooms she sometimes had use of, while Whitney Houston singing "I will always love you" blared from the room below and the couple above her were arguing noisily as usual. She could hear every single word they shouted and she knew their dialogue by heart. It was the same every afternoon when he returned from the pub. The sound of items of furniture being thrown no longer perturbed her. It was all so familiar.

So was the feeling of lethargy that threatened to engulf her. Could she face going out, working tonight? She sighed, knowing the answer. She needed the money and she needed to see the other girls. Sometimes they had a real laugh together when there were no men around. Although that was rare – most of them had boyfriends who were their pimps. Princess had never had a boyfriend and had no pimp either but she did pay a couple of all-night car park attendants to come to her aid should the need arise. These days you could never be sure.

Look at Lisa. She was the nearest thing to a best friend and now she was dead. Princess had heard about her death from Sam on the afternoon of the interview. He'd been questioned for three hours, though none of the women could think why. No one could suspect Sam. Princess hadn't worked that night. Now she felt cold in spite of the heat in the room and lit another cigarette. The ashtray was already full. She inhaled deeply.

She knew Lisa had been made an offer she couldn't refuse, something to do with the guy who cruised round in the black Merc. Lisa wasn't the only one. At the time, Princess had felt quite jealous but now... She had been found dead and Princess was ready to bet that that driver had something to do with it. She'd asked around and she was sure Mimi had also been approached. And she hadn't seen Mimi for weeks. Nor Tracey.

The police seemed to be looking the other way. *If they didn't spend so much bleeding time nicking us, they might solve a few real crimes,* Princess thought, *that is if they aren't up to their ears in it themselves.*

Stretching her limbs, she turned her attention back to the red exercise book she had been writing in. It had become like a drug with her now – writing – and she re-read what she had just penned:

I keep having nightmares. I keep dreaming about Frank. When he raped me. You'd think after all the men I've fucked, it wouldn't make any difference. But it does. It still hurts, remembering...

TEN

Caroline was drying herself in the bathroom. It was 2.30 in the afternoon and it was bliss having the place to herself. In fact, since soon after Frank had moved in, she only ever had a bath when the flat was empty. She hated the way he was always watching her, or rubbing up against her when her mother wasn't looking. He always made the excuse that he needed to pee when she was in the bath so she stopped bathing when he was around.

She'd bunked off school and crept back into the flat after her mother had set off for work and Frank had left for the pub. Now the radio was turned up full and she was singing along to Diana Ross's "Chain Reaction", Capital Radio's current number one. Caroline cupped her budding breasts and admired them in the mirror on the opposite wall. Then she thought of her mother's pendulous pair. If that's what having kids did for you…

Suddenly she had the uncanny sensation of being watched. Caroline turned off the radio. "Hel-lo?" she called into the silence. The hinges on the bathroom door creaked in protest as the door was flung back to reveal Frank, a horrible leer on his face. With one hand he reached out and grabbed Caroline's shoulder while his other hand stroked his erect penis, which stuck out grotesquely from his open flies.

"You've been waiting for this, haven't you, you little bitch?" Frank's fingers were biting into her flesh.

"Get out!" Caroline shrieked.

Frank didn't move. "I've seen you bunking off with your little boyfriends, you dirty little whore."

"Don't you dare touch me! I'll tell mum!"

The slap across her face sounded like the crack of the whip. "You tell no one, right? No one or I'll do fer yer and yer bleedin' mother, right?" He grabbed her hair and yanked it viciously to emphasis his point. Caroline screamed out in agony and in that moment Frank bent her head forward and thrust himself into her mouth.

Caroline gagged; she was suffocating. She struggled but her efforts seemed to excite him more and there was little she could do against a man more than twice her weight. *Bite him.* Just as the thought came into her mind, Frank, anticipating her, removed his swollen organ.

"Not so fast, bitch," he whispered into her face, his foul breath making her retch before an even worse assault on her body made her scream out. Frank pushed her to the floor and rammed his penis into her. She thought she was being torn apart. The pain. On and on it seemed to go on forever as he pinched her nipple, bit into her breast and pounded his dreadful weight over and on her. Just when she thought she would die, Frank let out a terrible groan and collapsed onto her. She thought he was dead, then realised he was still breathing.

A few moments later, he rolled off her and Caroline just made it to the toilet before vomiting violently. She could sense Frank standing behind. "You can clear up that mess as well, you hear."

Caroline glanced down to where he was pointing at the blood on the floor. She was aware of something trickling between her legs and felt her stomach retch in revolt as she noticed the blood smeared on her legs. The room span and her childhood was over.

◊ ◊ ◊

Friday 9 July, 1993

I did tell my mum. Mum didn't believe me. She called me a liar. Said I'd never liked Frank and was always trying to spoil things for her. I hated her then. I still hate her. She's done this to me. It's all her fault.

Then I missed a period and found out I was pregnant. My mum called me a whore and a bitch but she didn't believe it was Frank's or that he'd raped me. Mum took me to social services. They got rid of the baby. I was glad. I didn't want that pig's child.

I thought I'd be safe in the children's home. I was from Frank. But not from the boys or the staff. I was on the pill by then…

"Oh shit!" Princess jumped up and grabbed her handbag – searching inside for the packet. She stared at it in dismay. Yesterday's pill was the third she'd missed this month.

"Fuck." She took two for good measure then made herself a cup of tea. Whatever she'd told that journalist, she did sometimes do it without a rubber. Not often. Only when she thought the punter was safe – a nice married man – or when she was desperate for extra cash. Some men would pay double for it without a rubber.

"That's all I need," she said to the pristine bride doll sitting on the table by her bed. She rearranged the folds of the long white dress before turning her less careful but more creative attentions to herself.

ELEVEN

The closing credits rolled. Hannah picked up the remote and rewound the video. She'd recorded the programme and had watched it twice. She hadn't been impressed with the documentary. It was superficial; the programme makers should have come up with something more original after spending nearly three months at King's Cross. The women came across as set piece stereotypes, everybody's idea of a hooker – cheap, tarty, over made up and not too intelligent. The police emerged as caring social workers with a sense of humour and a conscience. Tom Jordan spoke off camera most of the time, but when he did appear on-screen, he looked a bit too squeaky clean. *You'd learn more about prostitution at King's Cross from watching "Mona Lisa"*. Hannah thought dismissively. The film had been a favourite of hers.

Hannah's mind went back to Kathy Osbourn; she'd sensed the researcher had felt rather superior to print journalists, but if this was all she could come up with …

The whole programme was a dream come true for a certain type of viewer: voyeuristic. There were far too many shots of cleavages and stocking tops, women standing around under neon signs waiting for trade. Hannah wondered how these women felt when they saw themselves exhibited in such a way. Had they been paid for their time? Or rather had they been paid enough? It still galled Hannah that Princess had only been paid £100 for her story. She learned later that Kathy been paid for her time, although she didn't know how much. *That makes her no better than a pimp,* Hannah thought. *And what does that make you?* asked a voice she would rather have ignored.

She was saved from answering her own question by the telephone ringing. Hannah picked it up. "Hello." There was a long silence. "Hel-lo." The line clicked and went dead. Hannah slammed down the receiver, her face flushed with anger. *I hope all that business isn't going to start again, it's so bloody irritating* – and alarming, she had to admit. She'd had a series of nuisance calls just after the baby was born. If the answerphone was on, the caller just let the tape run and Hannah would hear various background noises – other phones ringing, typewriters, sometimes traffic, a train station announcement. It was all so pointless. And then it stopped. It had crossed her mind that Paul was making the calls, that he hadn't had the guts to talk to her. Surely even he wouldn't be so crass? But Hannah couldn't think of anyone else who might want to upset her.

In fact, she'd been surprised at how much the calls had distressed her. It was probably the relentlessness of them and the fact that she didn't know why someone was making them. What possible thrill could be gained in making so many calls and saying nothing? Presumably these tactics gave a weird sort of power to the impotent.

Hannah shook her head and blinked as if to rid her mind of unwanted thoughts and turned her attention back to the programme she was now fast-forwarding. It had had a depressing effect on her. Prostitutes depressed her. She felt uneasy about her own role. And there was a sense of there but for the grace of God…

She stopped the tape where Princess had appeared. No one would have recognised her from this. Hannah had missed her on the first viewing. She was filmed in shadows. What you did glimpse of her was dull hair and listless eyes; even the gravelly voice sounded different, lifeless. Nothing of her appalling past had escaped the cutting room floor. She just came over as a girl who thought this was an easy way of making a fast buck. She looked so sullen, you wondered how she ever attracted clients in the first place. But this Princess was nothing like the raunchy blonde of the glossy newspaper supplement photos.

"No doubting who you are here," Hannah said aloud as she glanced at the magazine before her, open at the double page spread of her article. She wondered, not for the first time, if the girl's father or mother or any of her family had seen the interview. In a way she hoped they had. But what good would that serve? Maybe it would prevent them making the same mistakes with other daughters? No amount of remorse could compensate Princess.

The interview, Hannah was relieved to see, had been subbed sensitively. Nothing she had written had been changed drastically. It was a very sympathetic account of one girl's personal tragedy. Except for the photos. Pictorially, Princess seemed to glory in her whoredom. *In her mind,* thought Hannah, *she's posing for "Playboy" or page 3. Christ, it's so unfair. All that for a measly 100 quid and certain notoriety.* Hannah couldn't imagine that her "sisters" at King's Cross would be too happy either. You could say that the photos were no more than free advertising for Princess.

Poor Princess. Hannah smiled at the irony of the name, as the sound of her baby's cries imperiously called to her. She switched everything off and went upstairs.

"Here I am, baby," she whispered as she entered the dimly lit room. Soon the infant was nuzzling into her neck, comforted and reassured. Hannah felt at one with her child. It was salutary to think that this was probably the same way Princess's mother had felt when the girl was a baby. How could everything have turned out so badly? The little fist clutching her finger relaxed its hold and Hannah kissed the tiny fingertips. *I hope I never let you down, darling.* And for a moment she longed for her own mother, but couldn't imagine Daphne ever having such overpowering maternal feelings.

TWELVE

The fingers around her neck pressed harder and harder. She could no longer swallow the bile rising in her throat. Her eyes felt as though they were popping out of her head. Her skin felt hot, dry, stretched as though about to rip open. She had given up struggling. "*This is it,*" she thought, just as a blow to her stomach shot a searing pain up through her body.

"Oh God, oh God," the male voice rasped as the paroxysm of his orgasm swept through him leaving him utterly spent. For a few moments, he remained motionless. Then he rolled off the woman beneath him and lay on his back, eyes closed, until his breathing returned to normal. It was then that he noticed the body next to him didn't seem to be breathing at all. *Fuck.*

He pressed a small button by the side of the bed and minutes later the door to the room opened and closed. *Thank God he didn't have to deal with this alone.*

A lightly bronzed hand picked up a limp wrist and dropped it. "Not another one. This is going to an expensive mistake, you know."

"I know, I know. Just get rid of her will you." His voice was increasing in firmness and confidence. Then it faltered. "Oh for God's sake, she's haemorrhaging all over the place." Disgust was paramount. There was no compassion. He walked over to the bathroom where he washed himself meticulously, taking his time. As soon as he was dry and dressed, he nodded to the other man and strode out of the room closing the door silently behind him.

A manicured finger pressed another, hidden button by the bed and moments later two men in surgical green walked in and prepared to remove the body.

"Usual disposal, sir?" Their faces betrayed no surprise or concern. They were paid well not to question the morality of beating up prostitutes to within an inch of their lives and then dumping them back on their home beat.

"Hmm?" The man who had remained in the room seemed lost in thought. "Oh yes, usual place. Make sure she's not found too quickly." He left the room.

"Hoity, toity bastard," said the younger of the two. "Who does he think he is? We are risking our bleedin' necks for 'im."

"Yeah, well…"

As they lifted the body onto a trolley, an arm moved slightly and a groan squeezed out between swollen and bruised lips. The two men looked at each other, each willing the other to forget any vestige of compassion that remained in them. They rearranged her clothing and made sure all her belongings left with her.

"Christ! I need a drink. Let's get rid of her nearer to home. Knock off early for change."

"Y'er on!"

◊ ◊ ◊

Lead weights had attached themselves to her eyelids or that's how it felt as she tried to open her eyes. There was no part of her body that didn't protest as she tried to move. It took every ounce of strength and determination to get up on her feet. When she did, her head reeled and she threw up. She wiped her mouth with the back of her hand and leaned heavily against the wall. Her breathing came in shallow gasps. If she breathed any deeper, the pain got worse. But if she concentrated hard, she could just about put one foot in front of the other. She made for the streetlights and the sound of traffic.

Pausing every few seconds to catch a breath and lean against the alley wall, she made painstakingly slow progress. At one point her hands went to her waist. Her money pouch was still there. More importantly – her fingers slipped inside – so was her money. None of it made any sense.

She caught her breath; the pain was excruciating but she couldn't stop now. At last she emerged into the street and, miracles, there was a black cab approaching with its yellow light on. She managed to raise her arm and gasped out her address when the taxi drew alongside her.

"You sure you don't want an 'ospital, luv?"

She shook her head. The driver tut-tutted but they were soon outside number 11. She got out and handed a £5 note to the driver. Leaning in close to him, she whispered one word, "Wait."

"Right you are, luv. No hurry."

She was almost surprised to find the taxi still there when she came out of the house some minutes later, clutching a large bag. She had written where she wanted to go on a scrap of paper. The driver turned on the overhead light.

"Okay then, Dulwich it is." And he said no more until they reached her destination.

She slipped in and out of consciousness during the early part of the journey. However, dredging up every ounce of strength from a reserve she hadn't known she possessed, she was conscious when the taxi drew up outside terraced house.

Pain seared through her body with each movement, but she managed to get out of the cab and pay the driver, giving him way over the fare.

It was only when he picked up his next passenger, he discovered she had bled all over his back seat.

THIRTEEN

The incessant ringing on the doorbell gradually imposed itself into her consciousness. Hannah roused herself unwillingly. She'd fallen asleep in the chair with the baby slumbering in her arms. Very gently she placed her in the cot and tiptoed out of the room. Why she did she do that when the bell had failed to wake the sleeping infant, Hannah asked herself. Habit.

She looked at her wristwatch. Two in the morning. No one she knew would turn up at this hour. Her heartbeat quickened. Her hands were clammy. Disorientated she peered out of her own bedroom window which overlooked the street. The front gate was open but she couldn't see who was ringing the bell. A fox was walking stealthily along the road. Nothing else in the street moved. Lights were on in other windows in the terraced houses opposite but that was not out of the ordinary. There always seemed to be someone awake, no matter what time she looked out.

The bell stopped ringing. The silence was infinitely worse. Pinpricks of fear crept up in her neck. Her hands trembled. She wondered if she should ignore the bell or even call the police. She knew she could do neither. She would feel stupid. In bare feet, she crept downstairs soundlessly and peered through the spy hole in the front door.

Whatever she had expected to see in her doorway it was not the crumpled figure of what she discerned must be a girl. She could hear her own heartbeat resounding in her ears and tried to slow down her breathing to steady her nerves. Hannah unlocked the door leaving the security chain on.

"Yes." Her whisper echoed in the night. A moan was the only reply. For a moment Hannah hadn't a clue what to do. Then, not pausing to think about the wisdom of her action, she unchained the door and watched in dismay as the body tumbled towards her.

Hannah stepped back and stared in horror. She couldn't move. Seconds passed. Her pulse accelerated, thundering in her ears. She swallowed hard to quell the nausea. A hand grabbed her ankle with surprising force.

"Help me... Please help me." The croaked plea, barely audible, brought Hannah back to her senses. She bent down and gingerly dragged the girl further into the hall, then shut and locked the door.

It was only when she turned on the light and stared into the swollen face of the body on the floor that Hannah at last recognised her visitor.

"Princess!" She felt her stomach heave again. She bent forward and cradled the girl to her. "Who on earth did this to you?" In her immediate concern, it didn't occur to her to ask how the girl had managed to turn up on her doorstep.

"Throat," Princess rasped; the single word caused her to grimace in pain. Her breath came in short gasps.

"Look, don't say anything more. Take some deep breaths. I'm going to try and move you into the sitting room. Help me if you can."

The combined odours of Princess's trade and Hannah's fear collided in the warm air and permeated the narrow hall. Hannah closed her eyes for a second and wished the girl a thousand miles away. *What in heaven's name have I done to deserve this?* she asked herself, heaving the girl into an upright position and nearly falling backwards in the process.

At last they were both upright. The limp, battered girl leaned heavily on Hannah whose eyes suddenly focused on this mess of blood on the carpet.

Shit!

"Lean against the wall for a minute," Hannah said more calmly than she felt and, taking the stairs two at a time to the airing cupboard in the hall by her bedroom, came back with the plastic sheet she'd had on her own bed before Elizabeth's birth and a bundle of towels and linen.

She turned on a lamp in the sitting room, covered the sofa with the plastic sheet and towels and threw a sheet over them. Very slowly and carefully, she led the girl into the room and lowered her on to the improvised bed. Princess winced as Hannah struggled to get her boots off and loosen her clothing. Angry weals on the girl's neck glared at her.

"Princess…" The girl's eyes strained to focus on her. "I'm going to call an ambulance…"

Terror filled bruised eyes. "No!" The word was no more than a croak but her face more than eloquently expressed her panic. As Hannah stared at the girl, she felt herself absorbing her alarm. Princess's fear became her own. A world she'd been paid to wander into, a world of crime, drugs and violence, had now come crashing inexplicably into hers. Hannah felt both pique and panic.

She didn't know how or why the girl had turned up on her

doorstep but… suppose she had been followed? The thought of heavies perhaps beating down her door, her baby asleep upstairs…

Hannah was immobilised by fear. Terror gripped her heart. "The police. I'll call the police." She realised she said this aloud when the girl gave a blood-chilling cry and tried to struggle to her feet.

"Please…" The word escaped her like a hiss.

Extricating her hands from the girl's surprisingly strong grip, Hannah felt a moment of utter despair. *What have I done to deserve this?* she asked herself again. She knew she should phone the police and have this girl taken to hospital. That was the sane, logical thing to do but looking at the gruesome figure before her, she knew she couldn't betray the girl, as everyone else seemed to have done. There must be a reason Princess had sought her out and she felt she had a moral duty at least to hear what she had to say – if she could articulate anything, which Hannah seriously doubted.

With a supreme effort she willed herself to calm down, she took the girl's hand gently in her own. "I'll call a friend of mine. He's a doctor –" Princess's hand tensed in her own and she touched the girl's face gingerly. "You need medical attention," she said. "I don't know how badly injured you are and I'm afraid of hurting you more."

Almost imperceptibly, Princess nodded.

Hannah moved away to a table where the phone resided and pressed a preset number. The ringing went on and on. *Please God let him be there,* Hannah – who didn't believe in the God she was exhorting – prayed ardently.

Come on, come on, answer it!
"3492."

"James, I'm really sorry to wake you. I need your help."

"Hannah! What on earth…?" James, used to being wakened throughout the night while he was on call, was instantly alert.

"Please come round. I've got a – friend – here who's in a really bad way."

"Hannah, it's 2.30 in the morning. Can't you call an ambulance?"

"No. I'll explain everything later. Please James. I wouldn't ask if it wasn't an emergency."

She heard James swear under his breath but knew he would be with her in minutes; he lived in street parallel to Hannah's. She turned to say something to Princess. The girl looked only half conscious. Hannah felt inadequate and an overpowering sense of despair. She covered the girl with a large bath sheet and walked out of the room.

FOURTEEN

Attacking the dark stain on the carpet, Hannah tried not to think of anything but the task in hand. Since having Elizabeth, she obsessed about keeping floors where the baby might crawl, clean. Now she worked to remove the blemish, concentrating on the spot rather than its author. She was in the kitchen, pouring bleach into the sink when there was a short ring on the bell.

Wearing a faded tracksuit and carrying a battered, bulging bag, James filled the hallway. He looked every inch the amateur rugby player he was and was very definitely not pleased. Hannah, who had known him since he moved into the flat she sold to buy her house, had never seen him quite so angry. On the other hand, she had never woken him at 2.30 in the morning either.

"Where is she?" He said abruptly and followed Hannah into the sitting room; she wondered why he'd assumed it was a woman.

"Jesus, Hannah! What's going on?" James's gaze took in the prostrate girl and the woman he'd grown to love like a sister and couldn't begin to see a connection. He was tired and confused, but this girl didn't look as though she'd be claimed as one of

Hannah's friends.

"I don't know what has happened and I can't explain anything. She turned up half an hour ago in the state. She is terrified and…"

"What's her name?" James's voice was resigned. He was already on his knees by the patient. His bag was open and he pulled on some latex gloves

"P…" Some uncanny inner voice urged caution. "Caroline," she said after a momentary hesitation.

"Okay, Caroline, can you hear me?" Princess, eyes like muddied pools in her distorted face, nodded.

"Right now I want you to open your mouth as wide as you can…" James's professional persona took over as he examined Princess expertly.

"Cut this away, will you?" he barked at Hannah. "Wait! Put on these." He handed her some latex gloves. It was seconds before Hannah realised the implications then immediately did as she was told.

The bleeding had stopped but there were congealed clots in Princess's pants.

"We'll need some warm water."

Hannah was glad to escape to the kitchen; her stomach was heaving. She opened a window and gulped in the cool night air before returning with a bowl of water.

Awkwardly, Hannah bathed between the girl's legs. It was such an intimate action between women who were all but strangers. Soon the water in the bowl was crimson and she had to change it several times before her task was completed.

James palpated her abdomen. All the time he was quietly reassuring the girl. He exuded confidence and charm and his patient responded with nods and an attempt at a smile, which looked so painful, Hannah had to look away. Suddenly in an ordinary voice James said, "Turn some heating on, can't you Hannah, it's freezing in here."

It wasn't freezing, but Princess was beginning to shudder with cold and shock. Hannah hadn't been able to find any sanitary pads so they improvised with one of Elizabeth's disposable nappies. James gave Princess a pain-killing injection and then, between them, they managed to get what was left of her clothes off, some old pajamas on and the sheet changed.

Hannah covered Princess with a duvet.

"Best to burn all this," commented James as he removed his gloves. "And be careful." He rubbed his eyes. Hannah looked so pale he thought she was about to pass out. "Oh Christ, bundle it all into a black bag and I'll get rid of it in the hospital incinerator."

"Thank you, I…" Hannah hiccupped, trying to stifle a sob. Now that the immediate danger was over, shock was setting in. James gave her a long look. He wanted to take into his arms but thought she might take it the wrong way. She was so prickly at times. Especially since the baby.

"She'll sleep for a few hours now," he said quietly. "When she wakes up, give her three of these every four hours to ease the pain." He handed her a bottle of pills. "There doesn't seem to be any major damage to her larynx so that'll heal itself but she'll need to see someone in a few days about her abortion."

"Can't you…?"

James was already shaking his head. "No, Hannah, I can't – and don't look at me like that. I'm just doing this as a favour – to you." The set of his face gave nothing away as he picked up his bag and walked to the door.

"I don't know what's going on Hannah, and frankly I don't want to, but I suggest you get rid of her pretty damn quick."

FIFTEEN

"And it's goodbye from Sue and me and all the Today team, we'll be on the air from 6.30 tomorrow morning..."

Hannah groaned. She'd overslept. It was a wonder that Elizabeth hadn't woken her. Then she realised that Elizabeth was snuggled up beside her. She couldn't remember getting up to her in the night. Thank God, Alex wasn't due in today. She was becoming more and more disillusioned with the part-time nanny and had started to dread the days she came in to look after Elizabeth. So, she felt, had her daughter. But that was probably transference of her guilty feelings at having to start work again so soon after Elizabeth's birth.

As the daytime world came into focus, Hannah remembered the girl who was, she presumed, still sleeping downstairs. Hannah wanted to believe it had all been some ghastly nightmare and would have loved to stay in bed longer. Perhaps the girl had left already? It was a vain hope. Princess had looked in no condition to stand up let alone quit the house unaided.

Hannah sighed. *I'd better get up in case she wakes and wonders where she is, she thought. Although from the look of her anywhere would be preferable to where she had come from. But how and why did she find me?* It was a question Hannah found unanswerable.

Elizabeth stirred beside her.

"Hello beautiful. Would you like some breakfast too?"

Elizabeth beamed.

◊ ◊ ◊

For three days, Hannah tended the sick girl. As luck would have it, she had no work on and Alex had phoned in with yet another feeble excuse. Last time she'd been "sick", Hannah had discovered she'd gone off to help her boyfriend on a decorating job. Hannah had only just made the deadline for an article she was writing and was furious. This time, she was relieved. She didn't want a witness to Princess's presence.

Princess said little. Hannah had installed her on the futon in the baby's room and had moved the cot into her own room.

When she woke that first morning, she looked nightmarish: make-up streaked across her swollen face. Filthy hands. Broken nails. Hair matted.

Half carrying, half pushing, Hannah had managed to get her up the stairs to the bathroom. She was going to leave her to it but she looked so pathetic, Hannah, daughter looking on from her bouncy seat, ran a deep bath and helped Princess into it. Gently she removed the caked make-up, then washed the blonde locks using the shower attachment to rinse and rinse and rinse…

By the time the girl was in a night dress, snuggling into bed, her hair a blonde halo, she looked so young and vulnerable, Hannah felt more than a twinge of guilt at the uncharitable thought of

Why me? going round and round in her mind. In the light of day, the drama of the previous night seemed less menacing. Her unwanted guest less of a threat. But even so, Princess was a complication and a presence Hannah could have done without.

Princess slept more than the baby. As she could hardly speak, Hannah left a bell by her bed so the invalid could ring if she needed something. Princess smiled, but never rang. She drank the drinks and soups Hannah put before her. The ice cream raised a smile that transformed the face, which was slowly with turning to its former state. But most of the time she slept.

On the fourth day, Princess appeared wraith-like in the kitchen as Hannah and baby were having lunch. "Any chance of a fag?" was the croaked request.

"You must be joking. After what you have been through?" Hannah was stunned. "Anyway, this is a strictly non-smoking household." This was said with all the self-righteousness of a reformed smoker. Hannah had given up her 20-a-day habit some ten years before.

"Shit!"

Stung by the ingratitude and impatient at having another person in her home, Hannah said tersely, "No one's forcing you to stay here. In fact, I don't remember anyone inviting you."

Princess's face was a picture of contrition. "Please don't chuck me out." The voice was even more gravelly since the assault. "They'll find me again."

"Who will?"

Princess remained silent, her expression gave nothing away. Her stance was guaranteed to exasperate Hannah.

"Who will, Princess?" Her voice assumed a school-marmish tone. The girl was still standing in front of her and was now looking distinctly uncomfortable. It dawned on Hannah, belatedly, that her unwelcome guest was still very weak. "Sit down," she said abruptly.

Princess sank thankfully into the seat. She pointedly ignored the baby who had immediately tried to attract her attention. Hannah told her to help herself to some food while she took Elizabeth upstairs for her nap.

When Hannah returned, Princess was sobbing soundlessly. "You did know that you were pregnant, didn't you?" Hannah asked softly.

"No." The girl's shoulders heaved. Hannah was acutely aware of her inadequacy as the bearer of bad news and that her own child could be a painful reminder of Princess's is loss.

"But you do realise you've had a miscarriage?"

Princess nodded. She blew her nose noisily into the tissue Hannah handed her. "I'm not crying because of that," she said jerkily. "It's just… It's just…" Another outburst of grief gripped her.

Hannah watched in silence. She had the uncomfortable feeling that she was being manipulated. She still didn't know why Princess had turned to her in extremis as it were and already she was regretting her hospitality. Princess's sobs were subsiding. Hannah handed her another tissue. "Come on, dry your eyes." Princess obliged rather theatrically, Hannah thought.

She produced a bottle of brandy left over from Christmas and poured them both a generous measure. "Come on, let's go and sit more comfortably."

Princess remembered nothing of the room from the night she arrived. Shafts of sunlight highlighted the frayed furnishings. Elizabeth's presence was obvious from the scattered toys on the floor and the photographs lined up on the mantelpiece. The room had an air of shabby elegance that was totally lost on Princess. Her idea of journalists was gleaned from films in which women writers lived in sumptuous luxury. This seemed all too homely, but when she thought of her own tiny bedsit and the loneliness, this was, in fact, comfort indeed.

"Why did you come here?" This question shouldn't have surprised Princess but she looked as though she hadn't expected it.

She looked slyly at Hannah and took her time in answering. "It was all your fault, wasn't it?" Princess sounded sullen and defensive. It wasn't what or how she wanted to explain herself and she was determined to win her over.

Hannah was very still. "What was?" she asked quietly, already knowing and dreading the answer.

Princess gazed at her, her expression inscrutable. "Everything." She twisted a strand of hair between her fingers. "It was your article."

Just as Hannah had feared. She wondered if the other women working King's Cross had taken their revenge. She sipped the brandy. "What happened?"

Princess studied her hair. "Pimps!" She spat the word. "They wanted me to work for them. When I refused, they came round and sorted me out, didn't they." She looked at Hannah mutinously, daring her to doubt her.

"You can't lay the blame for that on me," Hannah said thoughtfully. "You must have known the risks and you were paid for the interview."

"And that makes it all right?"

"No, of course not." Hannah felt exasperated. "It's a terrible thing to have happened. It's horrid and I'm sure the police will be sympathetic…"

"The police!" Princess snorted in derision. "You must be joking. They won't do anything. Why should they? Most of them are taking rake-offs themselves."

Hannah was silent. Princess was only confirming what she'd

already heard and suspected. But there must be some form of legal redress. The judicial system couldn't be totally corrupt. At least she hoped it couldn't.

"I'll have to stay here."

"What?" Hannah almost dropped her glass.

"I'll have to stay here," Princess repeated coolly.

"You can't." Hannah's face flushed crimson and it was nothing to do with a brandy. She was furious.

"Why not – you're responsible." Princess did not believe this, she just needed to work on Hannah's guilt – at which she was succeeding.

"I am not responsible for you," Hannah said through clenched teeth, "or for what happened to you. You landed in my doorway in a physical mess and I helped you. Not because I felt responsible for your plight but because I felt it my duty as one woman to another." Hannah pronounced each word with a precision calculated to leave the recipient in no doubt as to her meaning.

Princess, unabashed, changed tack. "I don't have anywhere else to go and I really need somewhere to hide," she said in a wheedling tone.

"Agreed. But that's not here."

"Why not?"

"Supposing they find you…" Immediately the words were out of her mouth, Hannah regretted them. She'd given ground, gone from the definite no to a possibility, which was the last thing she wanted.

"They won't." Princess almost jumped for joy but she sat still, pressing her advantage. "They can't."

"How can you be so sure? If you found me, they could too."

"But I had your address –" Hannah groaned – "at least I learned it by heart. It was on the envelope of money you gave me. I learned it then chucked the envelope, didn't I?"

"Well, that's something, I suppose," sighed Hannah, getting up to pour another drink. She needed it.

"So I can stay?" Princess sounded almost elated.

"No!" Hannah's voice rang out. Her hands were clammy. This was emotional blackmail. It wasn't her fault. None of this. She hadn't turned the girl into a prostitute. She hadn't forced the girl to do the interview. "Why didn't you go to Kathy? You seemed quite pally." Hannah hated the cynicism in her voice.

"I don't have her address and I don't trust her."

Hannah snorted. "And you trust me?"

"Yeah."

"Oh come on. How on earth do you know you can trust me?"

"I just know. You've got a baby."

"And what's that got to do with it?" Hannah barked, immediately defensive.

"I thought you'd understand."

"Oh, did you? Well you're wrong. I don't understand, and what's more, I don't want to."

"You've got to help me," Princess pleaded.

"Got to?" came the harsh reply. "What right do you have to barge into my home?"

"Please…"

Hannah looked at the girl; she didn't see a hard-bitten whore. She just saw a lonely, unhappy, unloved child. She thought of her own chubby baby and felt almost guilty at how much she loved her. Compassion got the better of her. Perhaps she could let her stay a few more days. *It won't kill me,* Hannah thought, *to have her here on a temporary basis.*

"We'll work something out," was all she would commit herself to.

SIXTEEN

Working something out included a new look for Caroline as Hannah now insisted on calling her. Once the obvious bruises had faded, an appointment with Hannah's local hairdresser at Village Way produced an auburn bob, and a pair of glasses completed the transformation. It seemed strange seeing the girl looking almost virginal, sitting in Hannah's home, reading Hannah's books and generally trying to keep out of Hannah's way.

Caroline continued to ignore the baby, at least as far as anyone can ignore a baby who spent her waking hours giggling and chuckling at her mother. She rarely cried. Hannah could almost feel Caroline's coolness. She would have described it as resentment. Maybe she was thinking of the baby she lost, but whenever Hannah questioned her, she seemed almost indifferent. She wasn't in pain. The bleeding had stopped. It was over, a relief.

Contrary to what he had said, James did come back to see Caroline. He examined her with Hannah in the room and then asked to talk to "the patient" alone. Hannah never discovered what was said but James didn't lose his worried look. He was obviously concerned. He'd taken a blood sample to test for anaemia and gave Caroline some iron tablets to take just in case. Caroline was obviously impressed with James and Hannah was left wondering what had passed between them. And a tiny, irrational part of her was jealous of James's attention to her.

Alex, the erstwhile nanny, had never come back. She'd sent a brief letter saying she'd found another job and returned the key, also asking for money owed to her for hours she hadn't worked. Hannah was furious, then couldn't disguise her horror when Caroline offered to baby-mind.

"I don't think so, thank you," said Hannah firmly, hoping the girl had only made the offer out of politeness in the expectation of being turned down.

"Why not?" Caroline asked quietly, pretending an interest in the magazine in front of her but covertly watching Hannah.

"Well, you've hardly got any experience, have you?" Hannah said dismissively.

"Did you?"

"I'm sorry?" Hannah immersed in the "Independent", wasn't really concentrating on the conversation.

"Did you have any experience of looking after babies before you had Elizabeth?"

"That's different."

"Why?"

"I'm her mother."

"Big deal."

Hannah, stung by the girl's tone, finally looked at her companion. Caroline's eyes looked a bit too bright and Hannah realised she had offended her. However, she didn't want to get into a discussion about childcare or Caroline's part in it. Caroline, she fervently hoped, would soon feel safe enough to leave.

"I've already made other arrangements," she said in a kinder tone. Someone I met at ante-natal classes is going to look after Elizabeth when I need her to. Her little boy is the same age."

Caroline sniffed but said no more.

◊ ◊ ◊

"Why didn't you get married?" Caroline asked one afternoon, watching Hannah playing with Elizabeth.

"It wasn't an option," replied Hannah, observing Elizabeth's frustrated attempts at stacking rings.

Caroline went silent for several minutes. "Why not?" she asked then looked as though she wondered if she had gone too far. *For a journalist who noses into other people's lives, Caroline thought, she doesn't like to give much about herself away.*

Hannah looked up and smiled. She was at her most relaxed when Elizabeth was with her. "Why not what?"

"Why wasn't getting married an option?" Caroline's vocabulary was definitely improving with all her reading and imitating Hannah.

The older woman sat back on her heels and looked at Caroline curled up on the sofa, an open book resting on the arm. "It wasn't that sort of relationship." Fleetingly she longed for the intimacy Paul had provided, even at arm's length. Whatever their relationship wasn't, it had provided fun, warmth and lots of good sex. It all seemed a million years away now.

Elizabeth crawled onto her lap and Hannah's expression softened. "When I discovered I was pregnant, Paul, the father, offered me money for an abortion and when I refused, I didn't see him for dust." Hannah's voice betrayed none of the emotion she had felt at the time. She had been stunned by Paul's reaction, although she had never expected him to be a full-time father. Their relationship had lasted so long because they both enjoyed their own company; neither of them wanted a conventional marriage and joint home. Amazingly, the pain of Paul's rejection was muted by the joy of carrying his child.

"Bastard. Didn't that hurt?"

"It did at the time, but really once Elizabeth was born, nothing else seemed to matter."

Caroline digested this. "But don't you get bored? You don't go out much, do you?"

Hannah smiled. "I haven't got much energy left for socialising. And a lot of my old friends appear to have lost my telephone number." Hannah paused. "Now that does hurt…"

Hannah gave her daughter a hug and she giggled delightedly. "We've got each other, haven't we?" She tickled the baby's toes. "I feel very lucky, privileged really. I haven't got much time for men." She directed these last words at Caroline whose expression was unreadable.

"Are you getting bored?"

The girl shrugged, "I miss the girls really and the excitement, but it's nice not having to look over my shoulder. I dunno what I want, do I?"

Caroline became addicted to daytime television if she hadn't been already – and writing. She'd bought half a dozen more red exercise books and Hannah often discovered her writing away, or chewing her pencil thoughtfully. She rarely crossed things out and thoughts seemed to be effortlessly translated onto each lined page. Hannah quite envied her.

"What are you writing?" she'd asked one morning.

"Oh, things," Caroline replied.

Hannah smiled. "What sort of things?"

"About me," she said in an off-hand way.

When Caroline had arrived, she'd been clutching a voluminous, shocking pink bag. It apparently went everywhere with her and she'd had the presence of mind – Hannah wondered how it had escaped the pimps but perhaps there was nothing in there to interest them – to bring it with her on the night of her attack. The red notebooks now lived in there. Caroline never left them lying around and Hannah wondered if she'd be able to contain her curiosity if the girl ever did.

Early on, Hannah had explained that she didn't have any money, she was living on an overdraft and couldn't support Caroline. The girl had grinned. "Why don't I pay you like a lodger then?"

"But I didn't think…"

Caroline delved into her bag, producing a box, which revealed a false bottom that concealed a wad of notes. For once, Caroline had pulled the rug from under her. "How about 50 quid a week?"

Hannah hadn't wanted to put their arrangement on a regular footing. Nothing could have been further from her mind. However, as the days stretched to a week, and then a fortnight, she'd been wondering how to broach the subject of Caroline's departure. On the other hand, she couldn't deny that the cash would come in handy. Caroline was beginning to get under her skin, although she hardly dared admit it even to herself.

Hannah found her impression of Caroline increasingly difficult to reconcile with her minimal knowledge of Princess. Had Princess ceased to exist? The smoking had of necessity, at least while she was in the house. Hannah wondered about drugs but hadn't seen any evidence. Her language was moderated, and watching her scratching away with her pencil, Hannah couldn't imagine her selling sex. But maybe that was because she didn't want to acknowledge the fact. By denying the past, Hannah could live with the present and not torture herself with images of a possibly disastrous future.

Caroline did not refer to her attackers directly. "I feel safe here," was the nearest she came to alluding to the reason for her being there.

She showed no inclination to explore the area, although she did go out on her own now and again. Hannah never asked questions; she was convinced she wouldn't like the answers. Occasionally Caroline accompanied Hannah and Elizabeth to the park. If they met anyone, Hannah always introduced her as the daughter of a friend who was staying for a while.

Caroline was always taciturn on these occasions. She made it obvious she couldn't wait to get away, acting like a moody teenager, which wasn't far from the truth. But because of this, Hannah had put off telling her about a dinner party she was giving the following Saturday.

It had been arranged ages ago when Hannah was having lunch with Joe Rawlington, an old friend from college days. Joe had been really supportive during Hannah's pregnancy, so much so that some of his friends ribbed him about being the father. Joe had been delighted. A closet gay, he'd never dared come out and Hannah had helped with the camouflage.

Now Hannah wondered what Caroline would make of him and, more importantly, what Joe would make of her.

SEVENTEEN

"So who are these people coming this evening?" Joe filled his pipe and drew on it.

Hannah winced as a cloud of smoke rose. Pointedly, she closed the kitchen door and passed Joe an ashtray without comment. However, much Hannah went on at him, he simply refused to comply with her no smoking edict. Hannah was glad Elizabeth was safely tucked up in her cot upstairs.

"Thanks." Joe placed the spent match in its intended receptacle. "Chris and Jane, of course, I met last time."

"Mm, they're always good company. I don't know about Sarah and Gerry Lacon though."

"Lacon. That name rings a bell somewhere. Where did you say you met them?" Joe was pouring wine into two glasses. Caroline was still in her room.

Hannah accepted a glass and they walked through to the sitting room. "Oh I've known Sarah for ages – professionally that is. I met her on a jaunt to Leeds years ago and I've seen her at press dos and so on. When I saw her the other week, I just invited her on the spur of the moment. It was strange. She looked – well – grateful, I think. She accepted, providing Gerry wasn't on call or something. They haven't been married all that long. And she's his third wife."

"And what does he do?"

"He's a doctor – with a private practice, I believe."

Joe passed no comment on this, although Hannah could guess his thoughts. He was very active in his local Labour Party. Everyone thought he'd make an excellent Parliamentary candidate but he would never put himself forward – he said he preferred working from the sidelines and behind the scenes but Hannah suspected it had more to do with his sexual orientation.

"And what about your other guest?" Hannah looked blank. "This mysterious Caroline who's staying with you?"

Hannah studied her wine glass. "Oh she is no mystery. Just the daughter of a friend. She needed somewhere to stay and I needed the money, so…" Hannah shrugged. She didn't look up.

"That's unlike you. I thought you hated the idea of sharing your space."

"Yes, but privacy doesn't pay the bills, does it?" She smiled to counteract the bitter tinge to her remark.

"As bad as that eh?"

Hannah nodded. "I just seem to have lost some clients. They think having a baby addles your brain or something. It's not true, of course. I'm much more disciplined about work now – and who I do favours for. The hardest thing is that people I thought were friends don't care enough even to ring. Not everyone of course." Hannah smiled.

"What about Sharon, you used to do a lot for her?"

"Well, I don't now. She – let's just say, she hasn't returned my calls." Hannah laughed. "Still the publishers were happy with my book on pregnancy, so maybe there'll be some more work there."

Just then, Caroline came into the room. Joe stood up.

"Caroline, this is an old friend of mine, Joe." Joe held out his hand. Caroline stood uncertain for a moment, then clasped his hand briskly before sitting down.

"I'll get you a drink, Caroline," said Hannah, who returned minutes later with a glass for Caroline and the bottle to top up her own and Joe's drinks. As she relaxed into a chair, the telephone rang. "I hope that's no one cancelling." She reached over and picked up the receiver. "Hello… Hello"

There was a silence on the line, then a click. Hannah looked thoughtful. "That's happening more and more now."

"Maybe Caroline has given your number to someone?" Joe noticed a certain look pass between the two women.

"No," said Hannah. "It started long before Caroline came to stay." *In fact,* she thought, *it started again when I first got the commission to interview her. Surely there couldn't be any connection?*

She was saved from further introspection by the ringing of the doorbell and the flurried arrival of Sarah and Gerry who seemed to fill the room with their very expensive presence. Sarah's dress shrieked designer and her immaculate blonde hair and make-up made Hannah, in a dress that was at least three years old and past its best, feeling distinctly shabby. Gerry's evening suit was definitely over the top for an informal dinner party. His accent betrayed his South African origins, even though and some obscure reason, he claimed to be from New Zealand.

"What would you like to drink?" Hannah's voice seemed unnaturally loud in the silence, which followed the introductions.

Gerry Lacon! Caroline was suffocating. The room felt stifling. Her hand had touched his! She wanted to jump up and hit him with something, anything. Her knuckles whitened as she gripped the wine glass, but she stood rooted to the spot. She realised that she was staring at him. His piggy eyes had looked at her only briefly before looking away as though she was of no interest to him. He hadn't recognised her – yet.

Caroline didn't know whether to leave the room or stay where she was. One thing was sure; Gerry Lacon must not guess her identity. Until now, she hadn't known his name. Would he remember hers? How on earth did someone like Hannah know him anyway? Then she remembered the connection was with Sarah. Caroline glanced at her. She was too bright – as though they'd had words on the way over. How much did she know about what her husband got up to?

Caroline was aware of Joe looking at her oddly. *Shit.* She tried to smile at him but her lips refused to comply. She swallowed hard and stood up. "I'll help you with the drinks, Hannah." She managed to get out of the door without her legs buckling under her. In the hall, she took a deep breath and wondered what she could say to Hannah. There was no way she was going to sit down and eat with that man.

She followed Hannah into the kitchen.

"I hope this isn't going to be too boring for you." Hannah spoke into the oven as she checked the chicken. When Caroline didn't reply, she turned to see that the girl was wide-eyed, pale and shaking. "What's the matter?"

"It's him!" Caroline hissed.

"Who?" Hannah was perplexed.

"Him. Gerry."

"He looks a bit of a bore, doesn't he?" Hannah giggled; the wine was having a pleasantly relaxing effect.

"No! Yes! But that's not what I mean." She paused then, looking every inch a child caught out in some misdemeanour, said in a stage whisper, "He was one of my clients."

Hannah was pouring the drinks. She froze. The girl waited for some reaction and then realised that Hannah's shoulders were actually shaking. When she faced Caroline again, tears were streaming down her face and she had to hold her nose to stop herself laughing.

"It's not funny."

"Oh yes, it is." Hannah was almost hysterical.

Caroline was desperate. "He might recognise me."

This had a slightly sobering effect on Hannah, but she still didn't see the problem. "He's hardly likely to say anything with his wife sitting there, is he?"

"No, but he might tell someone. He knows lots of people."

"I dare say he does. A Harley Street doctor."

"This is serious, Hannah." Caroline looked on the verge of tears. She had to make Hannah understand without giving anything away. "I can't sit through dinner with him, I can't. He might tell someone." She stressed the last word.

Hannah gave Caroline an indulgent smile. She thought it was highly improbable that Gerry, even if he did use prostitutes, had anything to do with pimps. But Caroline was clearly terrified. Red hair and glasses had transformed her, but she might give herself away with the careless remark.

"Okay, okay. Don't panic… Let me think…" Seconds later, Hannah had a solution. "Pop upstairs and pretend to be vomiting in the bathroom. I'll follow you up."

Hannah walked back into the sitting room accompanied by the muted sounds of someone throwing up. "A little too much wine on an empty stomach, I think." She smiled at her guests, watching intently for any reaction from Gerry. He looked extremely put out and Hannah could feel her skin prickle until she realised the reason. Joe had just been castigating him about private practice.

Hannah breathed out, willing herself to be calm, and handed out the drinks.

"Last year we went to Madeira." It was Sarah's obvious intention to change the subject. "It was wonderful. Every night we went out to local restaurants. It was really beautiful, wasn't it Gerry?" Sarah laid her hand on her husband's knee. He did not return her smile. "And we had a simply sumptuous tea at Reid's Palace Hotel one afternoon."

"Didn't you go there a few years ago, Hannah?" Joe, Hannah knew, had said this from pure devilment. Sarah and Gerry were a disaster. So full of their own self-importance, Hannah suspected they thought they were doing her a favour, gracing her home with their esteemed presence and was regretting her invitation.

"Yes, I spent a week at Reid's." Hannah smiled at her glorious moment of one-up-man-ship.

"How on earth could you afford that?" Sarah realised, too late, what an appalling faux pas she'd just made, but was saved literally by the bell.

Hannah went to answer the door and ushered in Jane and Chris gushing apologies and brandishing two bottles of Champagne.

Hannah's heart sank as Gerry and Chris took each other's measure. Dinner suit and short grey hair versus jumper and jeans and a dark pony-tail. A few words and the two men gave the impression of being diametrically opposed in every way; it was going to be an interesting evening.

In the kitchen, Hannah put the finishing touches to the meal as Jane explained the trouble they'd had with mini-cabs. Hannah hugged her. "Never mind, you're here now and I'm really pleased to see you. I'm not sure how much of those two, undiluted, I could take." They looked at each other and giggled. "Take these drinks through, will you."

Hannah followed a few minutes later. "Dinner's ready. I don't think Caroline will be joining us." At that moment she caught Joe's eye. He looked distinctly skeptical and she wondered why.

EIGHTEEN

"Frankly, I don't see how anyone in their right mind could have voted Conservative." Hannah was just bringing in the main course and caught Chris's comment.

"Well I don't mind admitting not only to voting for them but canvassing for our parliamentary candidate last year." Sarah's voice rose as she bristled with palpable indignation.

"Why?" Chris shot at her.

"Why what?"

"Why do you support them?" Chris's smile was pure malice.

"I don't have to tell you that. It's personal." Sarah replied lamely.

"But you must tell people why you support the party when you're out on the knock, as it were." Chris was like a cat playing with a mouse.

"Oh, of course." Sarah toppled into the trap.

"So, why not now? Why not tell me? Convert me?" Chris challenged.

Gerry leapt to his wife's defence. "Sarah doesn't have to put up with this sort of attack. Hannah, I don't understand how you can allow your guests to be insulted like this."

Hannah was momentarily lost for words. There was a hush as everyone was looking at her, waiting. "I didn't hear an insult," she said quietly, "and I think we are all old enough to stand by our convictions." She served the chicken in silence, and then everyone started talking at once.

Chris put his hand on Hannah's. "This is delicious. Thank you."

More wine smoothed ruffled feathers.

"Do you have a garden?" Sarah asked.

"Just a small one." Hannah forked food absentmindedly. She'd lost her appetite and the conversation was becoming deadly boring.

"Then you'll be able to have barbecues." Hannah groaned inwardly. "We often cook outside, don't we Gerry? It's such fun." Sarah announced this as though she herself had just invented the outdoor grill.

Hannah couldn't resist rising to the bait. "Yes, the last one I had was for 40 people." She caught Joe's eye and smiled innocently.

Sarah ignored her. "Gerry just loves donning an apron and taking over the cooking, don't you darling?"

"Darling" nodded, then praised the food. Hannah relaxed a little, but she felt her attention drawn time and again to Gerry Lacon. He was, she assumed, in his early 50s, older than Sarah. He obviously took care of himself and his appearance. His hands looked cared for and his nails manicured. He certainly didn't look the type to pick up women at King's Cross. He looked far too fastidious and was way too pompous.

When she had cleared the table, Hannah popped upstairs with some food for Caroline. The girl was writing furiously in her red book and Hannah noticed that one of the telephone directories and her A-Z were balanced on the bed. Caroline shut them.

"I borrowed them from your study. Hope you don't mind."

"I do actually."

Caroline, still looking pale, looked up. "I'll put them back where I found them." She couldn't understand Hannah's possessiveness.

Hannah knew she was overreacting, but she wanted to slap Caroline's face. How dare she. Her study was private – not a lending library. Her face was flushed and with more control than she felt, she picked up the books. "I'll put them back and I'd rather you didn't go into the study. I'd like somewhere to call my own," she muttered as she left the room.

Still fuming inwardly, Hannah was greeted with raised voices as she returned from the kitchen with the dessert.

"Of course I could, and would kill, if I had to." Chris looked as though he'd targeted Sarah as his next victim. She looked like a rabbit caught in a car's headlights as a hand fluttered to her neck and Hannah wondered what she'd missed. "Everyone is capable of killing – if they had to protect themselves or someone they love, for instance."

"Some of us believe in the sanctity of life."

Gerry's comment, innocent enough, defeated Chris's logic. He rounded on Gerry. "That's rich coming from someone who was involved in buying kidneys from impoverished Turks."

Joe nodded. He too had made the connection a little earlier.

There was an unpleasant pause. Hannah had had no idea where Gerry worked. She was waiting to hear how he would justify himself, but Sarah was the first to speak. "Oh," she said in honeyed tones, "Gerry doesn't work at that clinic anymore and I don't think…"

"You don't think anything," snapped her husband.

"Oh don't be so pompous!" Chris rushed to Sarah's rescue.

"That's it!" A puce-faced Gerry got to his feet, his accent even more pronounced in his fury. "I'm not staying here to be insulted. Come on, Sarah."

Sarah stood up. "I'll have to use the bathroom first."

By this time, everyone was standing, speechless. Sarah took an age. No one attempted to break the awkward silence.

"Ready." Sarah, lipstick reapplied, smiled brightly at everyone.

Hannah saw them to the door, not knowing what to say.

"Sorry about this." Sarah's cheek brushed Hannah's. "He really is the most objectionable man. Do be careful," she whispered, "he is a self-confessed murderer."

Hannah forced her face into a remorseful smile. "Have a safe journey home." Then she leaned against the closed door and let out a huge sigh of relief.

The rest of the evening was a post mortem of what had happened, which became more and more hilarious with each glass of wine. At 1.30, everyone left and Hannah fell into bed only to be woken a few hours later by Elizabeth.

NINETEEN

Hannah had a major hangover the following morning and was glad that Caroline made herself scarce. It was all she could do to keep Elizabeth entertained. She was relieved when the girl put her head round the sitting room door to say that she was going out. And, still feeling distinctly the worse for wear, she didn't even bother to ask where the girl was going.

As soon as she left the house, Caroline made for the newsagent's across the road and bought an A-Z and a packet of cigarettes. She lit one and inhaled deeply before making her way to the minicab office a few shops along.

"How much to Mayfair?" She asked the female operator.

"Nine quid, love."

Caroline had only £10.50 left on her; she'd have to do a bit of business later. "Okay. Got someone who can take me now?"

"Ben… You've got a fare," the woman shouted to a man sitting in another room.

In the cab, Caroline put on her make-up and a blond curly wig. She wasn't sure what she was going to do, but it was time for some action and Mayfair seemed as good a place as any to begin. With a bit of luck, she'd be able to pick up some trade as well.

TWENTY

Three rings. "Hannah Weybridge."

"Oh good, I haven't got an answerphone." The voice was unfamiliar. "It's Tom Jordan." This was met with silence. "I'm the DI you interviewed at King's Cross."

Hannah came back to the present, "Sorry you caught me in the middle of working on a story and I was miles away. What can I do for you, Tom?"

"Well I just rang to congratulate you on the article you wrote."

"But that was weeks ago."

"I know but I've been really busy.

The was a pause, Hannah was wondering what the point of the conversation was when Tom said, "Sorry I was just using it as an excuse to ring and invite you for a drink and pick your brains."

"Oh I don't think…"

"Don't tell me you don't socialise with people you interview."

"No… but it's a bit difficult finding babysitters." Hannah knew her excuse sounded feeble.

"What about lunch then?" Tom suggested. "You obviously have

someone to look after the child when you're working."

"Ye-es." Hannah felt pushed into the metaphorical corner.

"How about the day after tomorrow then? One o'clock, Joe Allen's, Covent Garden?"

The element of surprise robbed Hannah of a ready excuse. "Okay, thank you. See you there."

◊ ◊ ◊

Hannah had gone down to the sitting room after the phone call. It had unsettled her. She was suspicious. Why had he phoned her now? It was the Monday after the dinner party and some of Caroline's paranoia had rubbed off. Although the prostitute's equilibrium seemed restored. Whatever she'd been up to the day before had had a positive effect on her.

Hannah wished she could say the same of herself. Her nerves were on edge and Caroline was like a constant itch she couldn't quite reach. The girl's reaction on Saturday was curious. There was something that didn't ring true. Caroline was obviously terrified, but Hannah wondered again about Gerry being one of her clients. It didn't add up. However, the fact that Caroline was beaten up when she arrived at Hannah's was indisputable. But were the perpetrators still looking for her? And who were they?

"Do you know a policeman called Tom Jordan?" she asked.

"Who doesn't? The crusading copper!"

Hannah laughed. "Is he straight?"

Caroline pulled a face. "Why do you ask?"

"I interviewed him when I interviewed you. He's invited me to lunch." Under cover of examining her nails, Hannah watched Caroline's reaction.

"So?" She shrugged. "P'raps he fancies you?"

Hannah wanted to scream. "So you don't think it's a bit strange that I get a call from him so soon after Gerry was here?"

Caroline's face was expressionless.

"Do I have to spell it out for you?" Hannah's tone could have cut glass.

Caroline's face registered a dawning understanding.

Hannah's patience was like strung-out elastic, which was about to snap. "Look –" her voice rose perilously – "you won't tell me anything about your assault. You claim, without any evidence, that an acquaintance's husband was one of your clients and could have recognised you here. By some quirk of fate, he's bound to tell someone where you are. Presumably the same someone who beat you up in the first place, but how or why Gerry should be in league with pimps, I fail to fathom. And you expect me to sit here and wait calmly for all hell to break loose on my doorstep and threaten my baby, my very existence, and not do something."

Caroline just stared. She'd never seen Hannah quite so angry. It suited her. She was too uptight most of the time. Then Elizabeth's cries filled the room via the baby monitor.

"Oh shit!" Hannah stormed out of the room.

When she returned carrying a beaming Elizabeth, she was calmer. Caroline watched her carefully.

"Sorry." Hardly an adequate response.

"I want you out of here." Hannah's voice was cold and hard. She sat down, and put the baby on the play mat. "I just can't take any more."

Caroline took two steps across the room and knelt in front of her. "Please don't chuck me out yet," she pleaded. "You've been so good to me. This is the nearest thing to home-life I've ever had."

"Stop playing on my sympathies."

"It's true. I feel really safe here."

"What, in spite of seeing Gerry?"

"Yes. I don't think he realised who I was. I can see the funny side now."

Hannah ran her hand through her hair. "Well I can't. I can't stand the tension and I don't like having someone else living in my home."

"I've tried to keep out of your way."

Hannah sighed. "I know. I know, but it's just too much of a strain. Look, I won't just throw you out. But we must discuss what you are going to do, now, with your life."

"I don't want to go back on the streets." Caroline's lower lip trembled as though she were about to cry. An art she'd often put to good effect with clients. "I just can't face it after what happened."

Hannah reached out and stroked the girl's hair. "I'm not that much of a bitch. I'll help you find somewhere else. But we also need to find out if anyone is looking for you."

"Perhaps they thought I was dead when they left me."

Hannah looked at her closely. "Then they would have expected a body to be found, surely?"

"Maybe."

"And somebody else must be missing you." Hannah was beginning to lose patience again. "Women working at King's Cross? Friends?"

Caroline bit her lip.

"Well, what about that community worker friend of yours? What's his name – Tony? Tony Vitello. Maybe he could help?" Hannah waited for a reaction. She'd had her suspicions about him when she'd interviewed Princess.

"I don't know where he is."

"Maybe I could find him," Hannah suggested.

"No!" the vehemence of the reply surprised both women and

the baby, playing with her stacking cups, jumped. Caroline leaned forward and tentatively stroked Elizabeth's hand. "Sorry, little one." Hannah couldn't help feeling the action was contrived.

Caroline moved and sat down on the sofa. *I need more time.* "Please don't throw me out yet." Her expression was earnest and guileless. "I've thought a lot about Tony since you interviewed me. You made me wonder if he knew about Gaynor. You know, her being a lesbian and everything." She paused. Tears threatened. "I trusted him… I trusted him. I thought he wanted to help me." Her gravelly voice had risen precariously, ending in a sob that sounded more like a snort. She sniffed noisily.

"Oh, do stop sniveling." Hannah aimed a box of tissues at her. "Blow your nose." Hannah picked up Elizabeth and cuddled her tenderly. Caroline felt hurt and excluded. She wondered if it was deliberate. Hannah seemed to flaunt motherhood and she spent so much time with the baby. But Hannah's expression had softened when she returned the girl's gaze and Caroline knew she'd won a reprieve.

"What on earth am I going to do with you?" she asked, but her tone was kind. And a germ of an idea was already forming in her mind.

TWENTY-ONE

Jo Allen's was packed. Hannah paused at the door as her eyes adjusted to the dimmer light. She'd taken ages deciding what to wear. Her body had slimmed down quickly after Elizabeth's birth, but many of her clothes still didn't fit. She was now a different shape. She would have loved to buy some new outfits, but with her precarious financial situation she was loath to spend money on herself. Still, she thought the long-skirted cotton dress she had finally decided upon didn't look too dated. It was loose-fitting and, in this heat, easy to wear.

Just as a waiter minced over to her, she caught sight of Tom Jordan at the bar and joined him. He looked up as she greeted him.

"What'll you have?" Tom asked with a smile of welcome, which deepened the laughter lines around those penetrating, blue eyes. She liked his easy grace and he certainly didn't look out of place amongst all the media types who made this their lunchtime haunt. Hannah smiled at her thoughts. An inspector was hardly a Mr Plod.

"Oh, a dry white wine please." She eyed Tom's whiskey. "I'm surprised to see you drinking. I thought you were on duty or something."

"No, I've just finished an early shift, so I can relax now." His smile transformed his face into that of a rather cheeky schoolboy – a sixth-former. His fair hair flopped forward and looked freshly washed. He had a scrubbed and healthy appearance; you wouldn't have guessed he'd spent most of his working hours investigating the seedier side of London.

"Why did you pick this place?" asked Hannah as they sat at the table they were led to.

"You sound as if you don't approve." Tom laughed. "I find it rather amusing to watch people and they make a nice change from the types I'm usually keeping an eye on."

"I suppose they must." Hannah wondered when he was going to tell her what all this was about.

They ordered and the waiter arrived with a rather expensive bottle of Chablis. Tom grinned at her arch look. "I'm not driving and I'm rather partial to this."

Hannah smiled back, willing herself to relax. At the same time, she had the distinct impression of being set up. Tom wanted something from her and she had a horrible suspicion it would have something to do with her guest.

They were on to the main course when Tom said, a shade too casually, "What did you make of the documentary?"

"You came over very well." Hannah could feel her stomach tighten. "I don't think it did justice to the women, though," she added choosing her words with care.

"No I …"

"Han-nah!" The shrieked appellation drew both Tom's and

Hannah's attention to a woman who was standing two tables away to Hannah's left.

Hannah didn't know whether to feel relief or despair. Sharon Hardiman came over and kissed her. "Darling, fancy seeing you here. Where have you been?" Her earrings clanked as she turned her head to include Tom. "And who is this gorgeous man? Not..." her eyes gleamed in speculation.

"Tom Jordan." Tom held out his hand, saving Hannah from having to answer. His smile was cool and calculating.

Sharon clasped his hand, "Haven't I met you before?" There was a gleam of recognition in her eye.

"No, I certainly wouldn't have forgotten you." Hannah's wince at the cliché was almost visible, but Sharon didn't seem bothered. She gave Hannah a calculating look.

"Darling, we must get together soon. You look wonderful. How is er..."

"Elizabeth is adorable. Perhaps you'd like to come over and meet her," Hannah asked sweetly.

"Ye-es. I'll give you a ring." She looked from Hannah to Tom, then squeezed Hannah's hand. "Well, I was just leaving. Enjoy your meal. Nice to meet you, Tom. Bye darling." She kissed Hannah's cheek, leaving a smudge of lipstick and was gone.

"Phew." Tom made a face and leaned forward to remove the scarlet smear with his napkin. It was an intimate gesture and it irritated Hannah – made her feel vulnerable in an odd way. "Rather heavy-handed with the Opium, isn't she?"

Hannah laughed. "Yes, subtlety isn't her strong suit."

Tom seemed to consider for a moment, then asked, "Is she a close friend of yours?"

"No she's an editor I sometimes work for, or rather, used to work for. I haven't seen her for ages."

Tom poured more wine. "Well, I imagine a little goes a long way with her."

As he raised his glass, something that had been niggling at the back of her mind suddenly exploded into the foreground. "You're not wearing your ring." It came out almost as an accusation.

Tom looked at his naked fingers. "I'm surprised you should notice or remember my ring."

Hannah felt rather silly at her outburst. "It was very distinctive. I remember wondering about it when I interviewed you."

Tom looked rueful. "Yes I was pretty annoyed when I lost it. It was my father's. Still…" He sipped his wine.

"Why did you want to see me?" The time had come for a more direct approach; she couldn't bear this pussyfooting around.

"I wanted to see you again and… there was something I wanted to ask you about." Tom gave her a searching look. "Remember the interview with Princess?" Hannah nodded mutely. "Well, frankly I'm worried about her. She seems to have disappeared. I've asked around but no one knows or is not saying where she is."

"Maybe she just moved away?" Hannah could feel a trickle of sweat making its track between her breasts; her hands were clammy. "Anyway what's it to do with me?"

"It's just a long shot but I wondered if she'd said anything to you – something you didn't use in the article – but which might give me a lead."

"Why?"

Tom sighed. "Thank you." He smiled as the waiter cleared away the plates.

"Would you like a dessert or coffee, sir?"

Tom looked enquiringly at Hannah. "Just coffee please, black."

"Make that two thanks." The waiter slipped away and returned almost immediately with the coffees. Tom concentrated on stirring a spoon of sugar into his cup.

"They look worth more than a penny." Tom glanced up. "Your thoughts," she explained.

"Mmm. I was wondering how much I can or should tell you." He sipped his coffee. "How d'you fancy a walk in the park?"

Hannah looked at her watch. 2.30. Elizabeth would be fine with Nicky for a while yet. "Okay – I'll just have to make a quick call."

"Be my guest." Tom produced a mobile phone from his briefcase.

"Standard police issue?" Hannah asked.

Tom grinned. "No, I just love new gadgets."

The phone call quickly established that Elizabeth had had a good lunch, was now sleeping peacefully and Nicky was quite happy to have her as long as necessary. Tom paid the bill in cash and they left the restaurant.

The heat and light as they emerged into Exeter Street was almost overpowering. Hannah quickly donned her sunglasses. They fell into step, walking easily beside each other. Tom took her arm as they crossed Southampton Street and turned into The Strand.

This must be the noisiest road in London, thought Hannah, glad that Tom was happy to walk along without trying to make conversation above the din of traffic. They had to compete for space on the pavement with office workers returning after a late lunch and tourists who held up the flow of pedestrians, walking slowly, guidebooks open in front of them, necks craned usually in the wrong direction.

For the life of her, Hannah couldn't think what The Strand had to offer them apart from the theatres and, of course, The Savoy. The shops, now that the Civil Service Store had long since disappeared, bore no comparison to what was on offer in Covent Garden.

Tourism might be vital to the economy, but Hannah hated sharing her London, the streets where she liked to imagine her grandparents walking some 50 years before, as much as she hated the litter that abounded and the fact that these same shop-fronts became home, at night, to a forgotten but increasing population.

Two relaxed-looking constables strolled by them as they walked across Trafalgar Square and Hannah was sure she'd seen a nod of recognition between them and her companion. There was no reason why they shouldn't know each other, but it did give Hannah an uneasy feeling, which wasn't helped by the mass of sightseers and pigeons in what seemed like equal proportions.

Landseer's lions looked anything but noble with children clambering over them to pose for cameras. And the pools around the fountains were put to good use by footsore tourists. Nelson surveyed the scene from above, while anyone wanting to see him in the famous square would get a crick in their neck.

The air seemed cooler as soon as they entered St James's Park and made their way to the lake. "Shall we sit in the shade?" Hannah nodded and they found a spot under a vast tree. Tom picked at the grass.

"You were asking me about Princess," Hannah prompted.

"Yes." Tom's thumbnail split a blade in two. "She's not the first to disappear you know."

"Who says she's disappeared? Maybe she's just staying with friends?" Tom gave her an odd sideways glance and Hannah mentally kicked herself.

Tom appeared to be making an in-depth study of the overhanging branches. "This is definitely off the record and I shall deny telling you anything if you write something…" Hannah nodded. "She's not the first prostitute to disappear. There's been a news blackout on this, but so far three women who worked King's Cross have disappeared over the last two months and then their dead bodies have been found in one of their usual haunts some time later. Only the girls weren't murdered there. They were dumped there afterwards and they weren't a pretty sight."

Hannah felt sick. Her first thought was to reassure Tom that Princess was alive and well, but something held her back. He appeared sincere but there were bent policemen… Princess's story had never added up either, the only facts Hannah could be sure of were that she had been badly beaten up and presumably left for dead and she could vouch for the fact that the girl was alive. But could she trust Tom? She wanted to, but a small voice in her head warned her to hold back.

"I don't know how I can help you really. I've still got my interview tape if you'd like to listen to that? She only mentions a few people by name. There was some community worker in Brixton – maybe he could help you?"

"Do you have his name?"

"Tony Vitello, I think. Apparently he's a martial arts enthusiast."

"That narrows the field." Tom stood up and held out his hand to help her up. They were standing very close to each other. For a moment Hannah thought he was going to kiss her; she tensed and took a step backwards.

Tom looked at her with an unreadable expression, "Come on, let's have an ice cream."

Sitting downstairs on a crowded number 12 bus, Hannah went over their conversation again and again in her mind. What were Tom's motives? Why the lunch? Why not just invite her to his office and ask her about Princess. It would have been a lot quicker and cheaper. But expense didn't seem to worry him. Maybe he was one of those policemen whom Caroline claimed took backhanders?

He did pay for the lunch in cash. Not that that in itself was a crime… Surely he couldn't claim that lunch on expenses? None of it made sense and the wine, sun and movement of the bus had a distinctly soporific effect. Once or twice she nodded off, only to wake as her head jolted backwards.

She was greeted at Nicky's by the sight of two extremely happy babies lying naked in a shady part of the garden. The peaceful domesticity of the scene relaxed Hannah and she spent an hour playing with them while Nicky popped out to the supermarket. It was after six when they eventually got home.

Hannah put her key in the lock only to realise that the mortise had been locked. Surprised, she unlocked both. "Hello, we're home," she called, negotiating the buggy into the hall. "Hello!"

There was no reply. The house was too quiet. Hannah left Elizabeth, protesting loudly, in the buggy. The sitting room door was open. Hannah walked in terrified of what she might find. No one. Everything was as she left it in the morning. She went through the house, calling for Caroline who was very definitely not there.

In a moment of awful clarity, Hannah wondered if she had been deliberately lured away.

TWENTY-TWO

There was no note. Nothing. But the fluorescent pink bag was still in the bedroom, so Hannah assumed Caroline would be back – that is, if she had left willingly. Hannah didn't know what to think. However, there were no signs to suggest Caroline had been forced out of the house. She felt guilty that her first reaction had almost been relief that she had gone. Her home was her own again. But she couldn't have gone far if she'd left the precious pink bag.

Hannah was sorely tempted to look inside and part of her was surprised that Caroline had left it there, unprotected. Maybe she'd only popped out and expected to be back before Hannah. The bag held her attention; she had to admit she was curious. But that would be a gross invasion of privacy. She would have been furious if Caroline had gone through her private things while she was out and she had the right to the same respect.

Elizabeth by this time had howled herself to sleep and Hannah managed to pick her up and transfer her to the cot without waking her. She gazed for some minutes at her sleeping form and felt the familiar surge of love. The intensity of the emotion still surprised her. She had never felt like this about any man – even Paul. It was a physical, gut reaction for her and she wondered yet again how any mother could feel any less. Her thoughts turned to Caroline, so bitterly betrayed by the one person whose love should have been totally unconditional.

Where was that girl?

Hannah felt nervy and restless. She couldn't settle at anything. In the end, she went into her study and flopped into the rocking chair, which creaked in protest. She closed her eyes. Sounds from neighbours' gardens floated to her. Children playing, voices, music. The heady scent of roses wafted in. A normal, ordinary summer evening with people doing ordinary normal things.

But not me, thought Hannah. She rubbed the fingers of her left hand. Her initial irritation at Caroline's absence was mutating into concern, a nagging worry and there was nothing she could do.

The telephone rang. Hannah jumped and took a deep breath before answering it. "Mrs Weybridge?"

"No. Who's calling?"

"This is a company call," said the slightly officious female voice.

"Sorry, not interested." Hannah replaced the handset. She went over to the window and looked out. The phone rang again. Hannah deftly switched on the answerphone, then wished she hadn't as the same voice let out a torrent of abuse after the outgoing message.

"Thank you." Hannah erased the tape. Looking at her untidy desk, she decided occupation would be good for her and tackled the filing. She hadn't done any for months and it made her feel good when the tray stood empty.

Still no Caroline.

Hannah made herself a coffee and turned on the television to watch what was left of the nine o'clock news. She had her back to the TV, when a familiar voice made her turn.

" ...fourth prostitute to be found murdered in this area and we're very worried. Because of the nature of our investigations, there has been a news blackout up until now. However, this new development means that ..."

Rooted to the spot, Hannah stared at the screen and the concerned face of DI Tom Jordan. The screen changed to Martyn Lewis summarising the main points of the news. Damn! She'd missed it. Then the awful realisation hit her like a kick in the stomach. Another working woman had been found dead – and Caroline was missing!

Hannah rushed out of the room and managed to reach the loo in time to be violently sick. Gradually the bile ceased rising. Hannah stood shakily in front of the basin and splashed her face with cold water. All the time her mind was shrieking one word: *No!*

She was just drying her face when she realised she could now catch the ITV ten o'clock bulletin. She staggered downstairs and switched channels. Hannah sat through the first half until the newscaster's voice said "and police reveal that four women have been murdered in the King's Cross area. All that in part two after the break."

The commercials had just finished when Elizabeth woke. Hannah groaned. She tried to blank out the wails but, unused to being ignored, the infant's cries became even more insistent. Taking the stairs two at a time, Hannah dashed into her bedroom, picked up the baby and, talking to her reassuringly, descended the stairs and a more careful pace. She could have wept when she saw Tom's face disappearing from the screen as she went back into the sitting room.

She watched until the end of the programme but there was no further mention of the dead prostitutes. Elizabeth was out for the count after being changed and fed. Hannah returned her to her cot and then searched her handbag for the card Tom had given her that afternoon.

Hannah dialled the number of his mobile phone five times and five times was told that the number was not answering. Hannah wanted to scream. She dialled his home number with little hope that he would be there.

She was right. His disembodied voice on the answerphone told her to leave her name and number. She hung up then thought better of it and rang again to leave a message. "Hello Tom, it's Hannah Weybridge here, I've just seen the news. Would you ring me please? Thanks. Bye."

She thought of ringing the station but if he wasn't there she didn't want to get into any complicated explanations. All she could do was wait.

◊ ◊ ◊

Hannah woke with a start. She held her breath. Someone was closing the front door – very quietly. The lamp in the sitting room was on, the door ajar. Transfixed, Hannah watched the door move silently open. The only sound was her heart pounding deafeningly in her ears.

"Hannah, are you there?" the gravelly whisper was followed by a face peering round the door.

It was some seconds before Hannah could speak. Caroline tiptoed in. Without her glasses, and wearing heavy make-up she looked completely different. She reeked of cigarettes and booze. It made Hannah gag and broke the spell. Tears welled up in her eyes and rolled silently down her cheeks.

"I thought you were dead."

Caroline laughed. "What the fuck made you think that?"

Fear quickly transformed itself into fury. Hannah jumped up. "I'll tell you what the fuck made me think that, shall I?" Her rage was palpable. "I come home to an empty house, no note to say where you'd gone. No phone call. Then I hear on the news that a fourth prostitute had been found dead at King's Cross…"

"I wasn't at the Cross…"

"Ohhh –" Hannah was close to murder herself. "It doesn't matter where you were, does it?" she enunciated. "The fact is I didn't know. I was worried sick. Can't you understand that?"

Caroline sat down. Hannah's outburst had a sobering effect on her. She looked so young and vulnerable. "Look, I …"

"No, you look. Four prostitutes have been killed. Four! Three weeks ago, you turned up on my doorstep half dead. Are you trying to tell me there is no connection?"

Caroline sat shaking her head. The colour had drained from her face and she looked shattered. "Who was it? D'you know who it was?" she asked quietly.

Hannah capitulated. "No, I missed most of the news. Caroline, where were you? I've been so worried."

"I've been working."

"What?" The word came out like a shriek. Hannah couldn't believe what she was hearing. "One minute, you're begging me to let you stay here. You swear you can't face the streets again and the next you're off without a word…"

"I did it for you…"

"I don't believe I'm hearing this." Hannah stopped pacing and sat down abruptly.

"Here." Caroline handed Hannah a roll of notes. Hannah stared at the money then counted out 250 pounds.

"What's this?"

"You need money. So there's money. It's not rent or anything like that. It's a present. A thank you."

Hannah stared at her. "Caroline, I can't take this."

"Why not? My money was good enough for you before. It was all earned the same way, you know."

Hannah breathed in deeply. "I'm not criticising how you got the money."

"No?"

"Of course not, I ..."

"Don't tell me you've got another nice commission to expose some poor bleeder's shame and you don't need my fucking dosh, right?"

Hannah was stunned by Caroline's accusation and her language. One night on the streets had transformed her. "No, that's not right."

Nausea welled up again, "It's just that... Caroline, I didn't want... I didn't mean you to ... for me..." Hannah felt drained and out of control. Everything was going too fast. She couldn't think straight. Only minutes ago, she had thought Caroline was dead. Now here they were arguing about money.

"No well... look, Hannah, can we talk in the morning? You look all in and I'm shagged. Is it all right if I have a bath now?"

Hannah waved a hand. "Help yourself." She went into the kitchen for a glass of water, then dragged herself to bed, all emotion spent.

TWENTY-THREE

The ringing phone wrenched her from sleep. "Hello?"

"Hannah? You sound as though I've woken you up?"

"You have." For a moment she couldn't place the voice.

There was a throaty chuckle at the end of the line. "Sorry, I thought children always got parents up early. I'm returning your call."

Tom Jordan. Hannah sat up in bed and her mind went back to the events of the previous evening. "I saw you on the news. It was a bit of a shock. I wondered if it was ..."

"No, it wasn't Princess." He coughed. "Look I really can't talk now. Could we meet later?"

Hannah was silent.

"If it's a problem, I could come over to you?"

Hannah was about to protest then thought it would be a bit suspicious. "Fine, I should be in all day but give me a ring first."

"Right." Tom's voice sounded clipped. Maybe someone was with him.

"Bye." Hannah hung up. And went over to Elizabeth's cot where she was, surprisingly, gurgling contentedly. "Come on, little one. Time for breakfast."

The roll of notes was still on the coffee table where Hannah had left it. She opened the curtains and windows; the bright sunlight mocked her fears of the night before. Hannah placed the baby on the play mat with some toys and went through her post. No bills, a few circulars, press releases and a bank statement. She opened it reluctantly. Overdrawn but just within her limit. Her last payment hadn't gone in yet, so it wasn't too bad.

Hannah contemplated the envelope she'd saved till last and slit it open. She glanced at the few typed line:

Sorry Hannah, this one isn't quite right for us either. Keep them coming though. Regards Joanne.

The letter was tossed onto the pile with the others. Rejections were becoming rather too familiar these days. She didn't seem to be able to break into the short story market.

Hannah thought of the novel she was always meaning to write but never got around to. She was always amazed that politicians who, whilst complaining about the hours they put in at the House, found the time to write endless tomes. Discipline maybe. *There's no time like the present,* she admonished herself. She ought to do it for Elizabeth. The object of her thoughts suddenly lurched forwards and let out a cry as she landed on her chin. Hannah knelt down beside her. "I think it's time for someone's nap," she said as she lifted her up and rubbed noses. Elizabeth responded with a well-aimed poke in the eye.

By the time she came downstairs again, Caroline, looking scrubbed and rested, was in the kitchen making coffee. She handed a mug to Hannah.

"It's time we had a talk, young lady," Caroline pulled a face but followed her into the sitting room.

"I had lunch with Tom Jordan yesterday."

"Yes, I know." Sitting with the window behind her, the light made a halo round Caroline's head. She looked like any other teenager about to be hauled over the coals for staying out late. But when Hannah looked at her more closely she saw that she'd obviously been crying. Hannah didn't want to hurt her any more than she already had been.

"He's concerned about you," Hannah said gently.

"You didn't tell him I was here!" Caroline looked appalled.

"No, of course not." In spite of herself, she felt irritated at the girl's obvious lack of trust in Tom. She had her own reservations but... "He wanted to see me to talk about you." Caroline snorted. "He said you'd disappeared and he is concerned for your safety."

"I bet he is."

"Caroline, I think it's about time you levelled with me, don't you?" Hannah tried to make eye contact, but the girl looked away. "Four women – four! – have been murdered."

"I know, I saw in the paper, Lisa – and Mimi – was me friends, you know?" Hannah didn't but nodded. "An' I've seen the other two around a lot." Her eyes looked dangerously close to overflowing and she rubbed them with the back of her hand.

"Do you know anything about how they died?"

The girl nodded mutely. She got up and walked out of the room. Hannah heard her mounting the stairs and a few minutes later she returned with the voluminous pink bag. She dumped it on the floor and sat down.

"I may, I may –" she stressed the word – "know something about how they died. Something. That's all." She leaned forward and clutched Hannah's hand. "And I can't tell you, because if I do, you'll be in danger too."

"And what about the police?"

Caroline gave her a withering look. "You just don't know anything, do you? These people are beyond the police."

"How do you mean?" Hannah scratched the knuckles on her left hand, a sure sign she was feeling uncomfortable.

"These people are powerful, believe me." Caroline's voice was even more gravelly.

Hannah pondered this. Caroline was very naïve. She was probably easily impressed by men who wore smart suits and carried briefcases.

Caroline sighed. She leaned forward earnestly. "These people, they're judges, MPs, even a top policeman…" She paused as if waiting for the information to sink in.

"Tom Jordan?"

Caroline laughed, but there was no humour in the sound.

Hannah wanted to ask more. How was Tom involved, if he was? Or did she just mean that any investigation of his would be quashed by his superiors? That must be it. Tom didn't have a part in all this. It was too preposterous to contemplate. *Only because you like him,* said a small voice. Hannah shuddered in spite of the heat. Her hands were clammy.

"I don't know if Jordan's involved but I'm certain one of his men is."

"Go on."

Caroline looked at her uncertainly for a moment. "Lisa was always talking about this copper called Don. She said he was a right prat, but he never booked her if she gave him a quick blow job. I used to keep out of his way, but I think Mimi and Susie used to give him one too."

"You're not saying he murdered them?" Hannah was not as shocked as she might have been.

"No I'm not. But he's the link between them, isn't he?"

Hannah was silent for a moment. "But what about you, then? If you kept out of his way?"

"I just got lucky, I guess." There was no way Caroline could tell her that she'd deliberately set herself up in the hope of finding out more about the place where Lisa had been working. That she'd accepted an invitation to earn some big money. She sipped her coffee.

Hannah would have liked to shake her. Why couldn't she just tell what she knew and be done with it? "But you weren't beaten up by pimps?" She asked.

"No." The hoarse voice was almost inaudible. "I got into a punter's car and was taken somewhere. I was given a lot of money…" For a moment tears threatened to overwhelm her. The terror, the unremitting pain and violence she had felt and been exposed to then… She blinked rapidly and bit her lips.

Hannah moved onto the sofa and put her arms around her. "Don't say any more if it's too painful."

"Look –" the urgency in Caroline's voice caught her attention. "I've been writing it all down. I don't know what I'm going to do with it yet but –" she looked beseechingly at Hannah – "if anything happens to me, I want you to have these notebooks. Maybe you can expose them through the papers or something."

Hannah had often wondered what people felt like when they said their blood ran cold. Now she knew. Fear left a nasty, acidic taste in her mouth. Four women had died. She realised now that the perpetrators may have thought it was five. Caroline, she was sure, had been one of their intended victims. But somehow she'd survived. Did they know this, and more importantly, were they looking for her? Tom definitely was.

"And Tom Jordan? Is he involved?"

Caroline shrugged. "I don't know. The last one was," she said flatly.

"The last what?"

"The last inspector at the Cross was involved in all the rackets. They got rid of him, but…" Caroline's shrug was eloquence itself. "Even if Tom Jordan isn't in it, he couldn't do anything. Too many people high up would put a stop to him."

"But…" Hannah couldn't finish the sentence. Her mind was racing. She felt sorry for Caroline, of course she did, but she was furious with herself. She had no right, as Elizabeth's mother and sole carer, to commit herself to such a vulnerable position and she had no idea how to extricate herself. Whatever happened, she was involved.

"Does anyone know you are here, Caroline?

Caroline shook her head. "I'm not that stupid."

"And where did you go yesterday?" Hannah knew she sounded like an old-fashioned schoolteacher.

"Streatham."

"Streatham," Hannah repeated for no reason.

"Yeah, it's good for…"

"Yes, I'm aware of that." Hannah's thoughts were darting off in all directions. "Did anyone see you there?"

"No." Caroline's voice was sullen.

"Are you sure?"

"Of course I am."

"And what about the other women working there? I thought prostitutes were supposed to fight off any competition on their patch?"

A noise that was halfway between a laugh and a snort greeted that remark. Caroline grinned at her. "You read too much." But the grin soon evaporated. "I was warned off, but trade was so good last night that no one was really worried."

"Well, I was." Hannah's statement did little justice to her emotions of the previous evening. "I think you need somewhere safer to stay. Somewhere away from harm and temptation." An idea she had been flirting with blossomed. "I know a vicar…"

Caroline almost spat her coffee. "You've got to be joking!"

"I know a vicar," Hannah repeated, "who lives in a relatively large village in Essex. It would be an ideal place and he's used to waifs and strays."

"Thanks."

"I'm sorry, I didn't mean that to sound the way it did."

Caroline said nothing.

"I interviewed him a few months ago. He's a very kind man. Not a holier than thou type at all. In fact, his wife's an ex drug addict."

None of this cut any ice with Caroline. "They're a sympathetic couple and I know you'll be safe with them. No one will think of looking for you there, there's no connection." She smiled at Caroline who had pulled a face at her. "And we'll have to work out what to do about all this… this…"

"Nothing! You'll do nothing!" The girl's voice was harsh, her face mutinous. "You can't get mixed up in it."

"Whether you like it or not, I am involved and it was you who involved me."

Caroline knew she was right but had one last card and it was a trump. "Think of Elizabeth." From Hannah's face she knew she'd won – for the moment.

"Okay, okay. I won't do anything for the time being, but …" Hannah stressed the last word, "… but I want you to do two things for me." She paused waiting for Caroline's agreement. She nodded. "Firstly, I want you to photocopy your notebooks." The girl looked perplexed, "I promise I won't read them but we do need to have a copy in a safe place."

Caroline could see the logic of this. "And?"

"And I'd like you to keep out of the way when Tom Jordan arrives."

"What's he coming here for?"

"To see me. I rang him last night when I thought you had been found dead. He doesn't know anything about you being here and frankly I'd like to keep it that way." *For the moment,* she added under her breath.

"So would I," said Caroline gathering up her bag. As she did so, something fell out and rolled across the floor.

Hannah picked it up and turned it over in her hand. She froze. For a moment she thought the world had stopped spinning. It was Tom Jordan's ring. Hannah tried to keep her voice at a normal level as she forced herself to ask the question she didn't want to know the answer to. "What an interesting ring," she said as casually as she could. "Where did you get it?"

"Oh some punter gave it to me," Caroline replied dismissively but she seemed in a hurry to get it back from Hannah. "Perks of the trade." She laughed and at that moment Hannah would have liked to ram it down her throat.

So Tom had lost his ring, had he? Hannah didn't want to believe that he had given it to Caroline. But why would she lie? If she could prevaricate so easily about the ring, perhaps she wasn't being completely truthful about other things. *Oh, what the hell have I got myself into?* Hannah just wanted to close her eyes and have the events of the last few weeks disappear. She watched Caroline walk out of the room. Was Tom one of her clients? Is that why he was so interested in her disappearance? It went against everything he had told her but why should she believe him? *You don't want to believe the obvious. And you call yourself a journalist.*

She would have gone on berating herself had the telephone not interrupted her. At the sound of Tom's voice, she blushed crimson. Thank goodness he couldn't see her.

"I can be over in half an hour, if that's convenient." He sounded tired and out of sorts.

"That's fine, see you then." The line clicked mid-sentence. *And what have I done to offend him?* she wondered.

TWENTY-FOUR

Caroline had gone out – shopping or so she said – and Elizabeth was wide-awake and at her most enchanting. Hannah watched from the window and saw that the inspector had driven himself over in an unmarked car. At least that made the visit seem unofficial or, just less official. It had crossed her mind that she could be charged with obstructing police enquiries. Her thoughts were cut off by a sharp ring on the bell and there he was before her.

"Hello." Hannah smiled shyly. She was immediately aware of how rarely anyone came into her home. How seldom she invited people. *For people, read men,* said an insistent little voice.

"Hi." He looked absolutely shattered but his smile was warm. More than anything Hannah would have liked to trust him. And perhaps she would have confided in him – if only she hadn't seen that blessed ring.

"We're in the sitting room but we could sit in the garden if you'd prefer?"

"No, I –" His hand reached out and touched her shoulder, Hannah almost jumped. "I could murder a cup of coffee, if you wouldn't mind?"

Hannah led him into the sitting room where she'd left the baby playing on the floor.

"Hello, who are you?" Hannah was surprised at the tenderness in his voice.

"This is Elizabeth," she said as Tom knelt down to take a tiny hand in his.

"Elizabeth, that's a lovely name, for a beautiful little girl. Is she named after your mother?"

"No my closest friend. She's a dentist working for medical charity in Africa at the moment so they haven't actually met yet."

"A joy to come, eh Elizabeth?" Tom wiggled the tiny hand.

Elizabeth was immediately won over and her mother left to make coffee.

By the time she returned, Tom was sitting cross-legged on the floor entertaining a delighted little girl.

He accepted the coffee gratefully. For a moment he looked haggard. "God, I needed that." Hannah suspected he was referring to his little game with Elizabeth as much as the coffee. She knew how he felt. Babies grounded you.

Although his face didn't register it, Tom had been surprised to see such a young child. "Are you married?"

The question startled her. It was the last thing she thought he'd ask.

"No." She rolled a ball back to Elizabeth not wanting to offer any more details. "Are you?"

"I was."

"And?"

"My wife died." It was simple to state that now. What he couldn't say was that she had been killed in a freak road accident and that his best friend had been in the car with her – both of them had taken suitcases. Tom had never found out where they were going.

It had been a triple blow and part of the reason he had changed careers and moved to London.

"I'm sorry."

Tom smiled and tickled Elizabeth's toes. "It was a long time ago." He stretched his legs and yawned. "I'm sorry I didn't get much sleep last night, one way and another."

"No I don't suppose you did." She bit her lip, hating herself for the subterfuge. "The girl…" Her voice broke. "The girl you found wasn't Princess?"

"No." He was watching her intently.

"And why do you need to speak to me?"

"Would you believe because I like your company?" He watched Hannah's expression of disbelief. "No?" He raised an eyebrow. "Well, I do." He made it sound like a declaration and his smile was warm and friendly.

Don't be fooled by this, Hannah told herself. He's buttering you up. She remembered the ring and hardened her heart.

"The fact remains," he continued, "Princess is still missing and could be, presumably is, at risk. I can't tell you the details but these murders have several things in common."

"One being they were all prostitutes." You didn't need to be a detective to work that one out.

"Exactly, but there's more to it than that."

"But why has there been a news blackout until now?" Hannah felt they were on safer ground here.

"I'm afraid I can't tell you that, either. Classified information – and you are a journalist."

They were both silent, taking each other's measure; Hannah forced herself to turn the conversation back to Princess.

"You say Princess is still missing. Do you think she could be a victim of whoever's doing this?"

"It's possible, well probable really. All the girls had been missing for varying lengths of time before their bodies were found."

"But why are you so interested in Princess?"

"Who says I am?" He smiled in a way that she thought was probably used to considerable effect with other women. Hannah wasn't going to allow herself to be so easily won over.

"Well, you seem to be. You invited me to lunch to talk about her. You…"

"Don't be so obtuse." He was laughing now. "If all I was interested in was your interview with the girl, I could have called you into the station or sent one of my officers round."

Hannah held his gaze and hoped he couldn't read her thoughts, which weren't exactly complimentary. She was convinced he was lying – or at least holding out on her. Caroline had his ring and he was looking for Princess, as he knew her. Maybe he was just worried that his very distinctive ring would end up on a dead prostitute's finger. But why did she have it? That was the million-dollar question and the one she couldn't ask.

She was relieved when Elizabeth's cry diverted her attention. She took the baby in her arms. Tom looked at his watch and groaned. "I'll have to be off, I'm afraid. No don't get up," he said as Hannah looked about to see him to the door. He smiled. "I'd like to keep that image of you both like that."

Hannah's wide eyes looked into his. He couldn't be involved. He was far too nice and…

"Oh, by the way, I nearly forgot to tell you –" Tom was standing with his hand on the door – "we found that friend of hers. That community worker."

Hannah swallowed hard. "Oh yes? Where was that?" But even as she asked the question, she had a terrible premonition that she knew the answer already.

"Streatham. But he wasn't very helpful. Rather a nasty piece of goods, I thought, still… I'll phone you later." He kissed his fingers and pressed them to her forehead and without another word was gone.

Hannah sat where she was, outwardly calm. But her mind was a whirlpool of conflicting thoughts. She went over their conversation again and again in her mind and realised Tom had told her nothing he couldn't have said over the phone. Maybe he had just wanted to see her as he'd claimed.

Hannah closed her eyes. Sitting in the sunlit room with Elizabeth snuggled into her arms, it was difficult to imagine that another cruel, nasty world existed. One in which the Princesses and the Toms where inextricably bound together.

It couldn't just be coincidence that Caroline possessed Tom's ring or that Tony had been discovered in Streatham just when Caroline had also been there. Both Tom and Caroline were lying to her. Of that she was certain. But why? Why?

She opened her eyes at the sound of a slight cough.

"Sorry." Caroline looked contrite. "I didn't mean to disturb you."

"You didn't." Hannah sat up straighter in the chair and looked down at Elizabeth who was mewing softly in her sleep. "I'll just put her in her cot," she said and left the room, glad of an excuse for any sort of action.

She wanted to be on her own – a luxury these days – and decided the bathroom was her best option. Standing under the shower with jets of cool water beating down on her body, rivulets running between her breasts, her hair sodden, Hannah felt herself relax slowly. She closed her eyes and concentrated on her breathing.

The sound of running water, birdsong and children's voices coming through the open window, almost blotted out the click of the front door closing. But not quite.

Damn! Thought Hannah. Where has she gone now?

Reluctantly Hannah turned off the taps and dried herself. Then it hit her. Caroline was supposed to have rung before returning, as Hannah didn't know how long Tom would be here. Had they met? Was she the real reason Tom had driven over here? Had Caroline been watching the house? Waiting for him to leave?

She was just slipping into a loose cotton frock when she heard Caroline opening the front door. At the same time, the telephone rang.

TWENTY-FIVE

"Han-nah, hel-lo. Stuart Grain-ger here. How are you?"

Hannah crossed her fingers hoping his call would mean another commission for *The News*. "Hello Stuart. I'm fine,"

"Good. Are you busy right now?"

"Not particularly." Hannah held her breath.

"Great! I've got something for you – if you can do it for us."

"Yes." Hannah tried not to sound too desperate. She was totally unprepared for Stuart's next question.

"Remember that prostitute you interviewed for us?"

"Yes." Her voice almost betrayed her.

"Well apparently she's gone missing, disappeared and the police fear she may end up a murder victim like the other four killed at King's Cross."

"Discovered at…"

"I'm sorry?"

"I thought their bodies were discovered there, but they'd been killed elsewhere?"

"Yes, whatever." Stuart sounded a little irritated. "The point is, the newspaper wants to do a bit of a follow up on her. You know, have you seen this woman etc… reward offered and we'd like you to use bits from your interview with more of your impressions about her and we want you to speak to the cop again."

Hannah's hands were damp with perspiration. She could feel the pulse in her neck echoing in her ears, louder and louder. She was caught in a spider's web and every move she made to extricate herself only meant she was more entangled.

"Han-nah?"

"Sorry Stuart, I was just thinking…"

"Think out loud… the news desk pays double feature rates, you know."

She didn't know and swallowed hard. Scruples didn't pay the mortgage. "Great, when do you want it by?"

"As soon as. Apparently the inspector is a little difficult to get hold of, but this is urgent. Rory on the news desk will fax you over a brief and you should contact him direct if you have any problems, though I'm sure you won't."

Stuart sounded more confident than he felt. They had been unable to secure an interview with Tom Jordan and hoped that Hannah could prevail upon him since she'd interviewed him before. And a little bird had told him that she'd seen Hannah having lunch with him in Jo Allen's. It was a long shot but if she pulled it off, his credibility on the paper would definitely go up.

"Okay Stuart, what's his number?"

"Extension 228. And good luck."

"Thanks. I think I'll need it."

Hannah was thoughtful as she replaced the handset. She was suddenly aware of Caroline standing in the study doorway staring at her. Hannah smiled. "And where did you sneak off to?"

Caroline looked hurt. "I didn't sneak off. I was just doing what I was told."

In reply to Hannah's raised eyebrow she said, "I went to that place over the road."

Bemused Hannah sat down at her desk. "I'm sorry?"

"I went," said the girl, smiling at her, "to photocopy me notebooks."

"Oh good," said Hannah.

"And I took two copies."

"That was very diligent of you."

"Well," Caroline looked sheepish, "the bloke in there was chatting me up. He's a bit of alright, isn't he?"

"Yes, he's very attractive," Hannah replied absently. Then the two women looked at each other and burst out laughing, easing some of the tension between them.

"Right, so where shall we send them for safe-keeping?" asked Hannah as the telephone rang again.

"Hannah Weybridge."

"Hi Hannah, it's James."

"Hello – you're still speaking to me then?"

"Just about." James laughed. "Still got your lodger there?"

"Yes, she standing right next to me," she said in the hope of forestalling any disparaging comments that Caroline might overhear. James always spoke loudly on the phone.

"Good, can I have a word?"

Hannah tried not to show her surprise. "It's James," she explained to the girl at her side. "He'd like a word. You can use the phone in the sitting room if you'd prefer."

With a hasty "Ta", Caroline disappeared down the stairs and Hannah put the phone down. The hum of the fax machine diverted her attention and she was engrossed in Rory's brief when Caroline bounded back into the room.

"Brilliant news!" she exclaimed as she promptly sat down in the rocking chair. She appeared very much at home and Hannah hoped she wasn't going to lose this refuge as well.

"It's negative."

"What is?"

"My HIV test, it's negative."

"Wonderful – but I didn't know you'd had one done."

"James arranged it for me when he took the blood sample to see if I was anaemic."

"Oh." Caroline's use of his name plus his consideration to her made Hannah feel unaccountably jealous. It was extremely selfish and childish but she didn't want to share her close friends with this girl. It niggled. She certainly didn't want Caroline to become an established part of her life. Hannah felt invaded by her presence. The sooner she left, the better.

"Well," she said into the uneasy silence, "I always knew he was a kind man." She smiled brightly and decided to change the subject. "Now, where are we going to send these?"

Caroline looked coy. "D'you think James would mind holding onto one for me?"

Hannah held onto the sigh that threatened to escape her. "I'm sure he wouldn't. And how about sending the other to the Reverend John Daniels?"

Caroline looked blank.

"The vicar I told you about. The one I think you should stay with for a while."

"Right." Caroline's expression was closed.

The author sealed the copies in envelopes, while Hannah wrote hurried explanatory notes asking the recipients not to open the enclosed unless asked to by Caroline or herself. Both women signed the letters and then they were packed into jiffy bags.

"Registered post, I think, don't you?"

"What's the difference?"

Hannah explained.

"I think I'll take them down to the post office straight away."

"Oh, by the way," Hannah said as she was leaving. "Your alter ego is going to be famous again."

Caroline looked at her blankly.

"I've been asked to write a piece about Princess's disappearance."

"Je-sus!"

"My sentiments entirely," replied Hannah.

"And you're going to do it?"

The journalist was surprised that the girl would even ask the question, but she sensed an implicit criticism, which irked her.

"It's my job," she said. "And it's money."

It could have been Princess talking.

TWENTY-SIX

While Caroline was out, Hannah took the opportunity to phone Tom Jordan on his mobile. It took her by surprise when he answered on the second ring.

"Yes," he barked.

"Have I caught you at an awkward moment? It's Hannah. Hannah Weybridge," she added for good measure.

"Hi." Tom's voice softened appreciably. "I'm up to my eyes as usual. What can I do for you?"

"Well –" Hannah felt reluctant to ask such a big favour but needs must. "You won't believe this, but I've been asked to interview you about Princess's disappearance."

"Oh yes." Tom's voice was markedly cooler.

"Yes. *The News* is doing some sort of 'have you seen this girl?' feature and are offering a reward for information."

"Hmm."

"I know you're extremely busy, but I thought as you were so concerned about Princess, you wouldn't mind talking to me." Hannah tried to keep the pleading note out of her voice.

Tom said something she couldn't make out to someone who must have been with him. Then: "Okay, on one condition."

"What's that?" *Please don't ask for copy approval,* prayed Hannah. She hated it when interviewees wanted to check what she had written.

"That you interview me over dinner."

"Oh, that's no hardship." Hannah felt light-headed with relief. "When?"

"Tomorrow?"

"Fine."

"I'll pick you up at seven."

"Great. I'll have to go now. Elizabeth's crying. Bye and thanks."

◊ ◊ ◊

"News desk."

"Hello is Rory there please?"

"Who's calling?"

"Hannah Weybridge."

"Right. Hang on a minute. He's just on the other line, Hannah."

Hannah hung on for about three minutes before she heard the news editor's voice.

"Hello, Hannah. Nice to speak with you. Did you get my fax?"

"Yes and I've arranged a meeting with DI Jordan for tomorrow evening."

Rory whistled. "Nice one."

"There's just one thing…"

"Ye-es." Rory wondered what stipulations the inspector had made.

"Do you think your crime desk could run a check on him?"

Rory was intrigued. "Sure thing. Any particular angle you have in mind?"

"I'm not sure really. He seems straight but you never know. And it does seem a bit strange that a British Transport Police Inspector is apparently leading a murder enquiry."

"Mmm."

"I've already phoned Scotland Yard Press Office, but you know how tight-lipped they can be."

"Only too well." Rory laughed. "Everything has to be a written request, in triplicate…"

"So you'll be able to do that?" Hannah interrupted.

"No problem. Anything else?"

"Well I'm going to try and talk to some of Princess's friends. I've still got the video of the programme on King's Cross, so I thought I'd attempt to find the woman she was interviewed with. You never know, she might know something and might prefer not talking to the police."

"Sure…" Rory anticipated her request. "You'll need some readies. I'll get some cash biked over –" Rory paused as if looking at his watch – "within an hour or so. Anything else?"

Hannah hesitated for a moment. "Yes. There's a community worker who was influential in Princess's life. Apparently he's now working in Streatham. I'd like to root him out. They may have been in touch with each other."

Hannah could hear Rory tapping something against the phone. "Yep. He might need some persuading. I can authorise you to offer to pay for his story… I'll send a contract over with the cash. If nobody else has got to him, he'll probably talk for £1000. If not, give me a ring. If I'm not here, speak to John Estry, the night editor. Okay?"

"Fine." Hannah felt a buzz of adrenalin. "Could I ask another favour?"

"Fire away." Rory was in a good mood, he was getting a lot more than he expected and if Hannah didn't get everything, at least she'd succeeded where he'd failed – in getting the DI to talk to her.

"Could you lend me one of those hidden mikes and recorders? It might facilitate things."

"It'll be in the package. Right I'd better get someone on to all this. I'll speak to you later and…

"Yes?"

"Take care, won't you."

TWENTY-SEVEN

"Streatham Advisory Services. Deidre speaking, how may I help you?"

"I'd like to speak to Tony Vitello."

"I'm sorry there's no one of that name working here."

Hannah replaced the receiver. It was the third call she'd made with no success. Lambeth Council had never heard of him. Nor had the Pinfold Road Information Centre. She could, of course, have asked Tom Jordan where he had found him but she didn't want Tom to know. He might try to warn her off or... Hannah didn't want to follow where those thoughts might lead. With the telephone directory open before her, she ran her finger down a column of entries. It skimmed over the *Streatham Echo* then stopped. It was a long shot but ...

She tapped out the number. "Echo."

"Oh er, hello. I was wondering if you could help me." She spoke hesitantly, not enjoying the subterfuge. It was a bit off picking a local reporter's brains.

"I'll try," said a friendly voice.

"I'm trying to get in touch with someone. I think I read about him in your paper a few weeks ago. Tony Vitello's his name.

"Oh Tony. Yeah he's always being quoted about something or other. He works from an office on the Tyneswell Housing Project. I have his number if you just hold on…"

Hannah held on to the phone and her breath.

"Yeah, here it is…"

Hannah wrote down the number and thanked him humbly. Well, that call saved a lot of work. She rang the number but it seemed to be permanently engaged. Time to put in a personal appearance, she thought. Her package from the news editor, Rory, had arrived. She fitted the micro recorder into her bra as per the enclosed instructions and rang for a cab.

The office of the Tyneswell Housing Project was on the ground floor of a four-storey block of flats, on an estate that looked as though it had never seen better days. The building dated back to the '30s and you could see similar blocks all over London. Most of the windows looked as though the tenants had given up fighting the grime that had accumulated on them, but in contrast, some had a sparkling freshness. The majority of the balconies had washing hanging from makeshift lines and Hannah thought the clothes probably smelled worse after their "airing".

A few youngsters clothed in the latest fashions and wearing, Hannah assumed, the most expensive trainers, were kicking a football around the forecourt. Hannah was willing to bet their parents didn't look half so smart. Disembodied voices from TVs and radios clashed and bounced off walls covered with graffiti, which dated back to George Davies's innocence and announced to the world, graphically, who was screwing whom. A few babies were crying. Momentarily, Hannah thought of Elizabeth then deliberately turned her mind back to Caroline and the elusive Tony Vitello.

There was a note taped to the door: *"Back in half an hour."* As she didn't know when it had been written, Hannah had no way of knowing whether she had the time to go for a coffee or if Mr Vitello's return was imminent.

"'E won't be long, luv."

Startled, Hannah turned to find an old lady had settled herself on a rickety chair on the adjacent balcony. Her smile betrayed ill-fitting dentures; her sparse grey hair was scraped back into a loose bun from which stray locks escaped from time to time, only to be tucked back in with surprisingly deft fingers.

"I saw 'im go off about 20 minutes ago, an' 'e never takes long for 'is dinner."

Hannah smiled and shifted her weight from one foot to the other. "Thanks. It's a lovely day, isn't it?"

"Mmm. You from the council? 'Bout time someone came to see about the drains round 'ere."

"Sorry." Hannah shook her head apologetically. There was a distinct smell of public lavatories about the place. The pungent smell of cheap disinfectant vying with something altogether more unsavoury.

"Pity, you look like someone who'd get things done. Still 'ere comes 'is nibs," said the old woman with a gesture of her chin.

Hannah turned to see a shortish, well-built man walking through the arched entrance. His curly fair hair was a surprise. With a name like Vitello she'd expected him to be dark. She hadn't dared ask Caroline what he looked like in case she got suspicious. Tony was one of the many angles she hadn't discussed with her "missing person".

Vitello looked at her speculatively as he approached. He took in her briefcase, short-sleeved dress and jacket and obviously thought he had her number.

"Mr Vitello?" Close to, he looked like the type of man you wouldn't like to meet on your own on a dark night. His appearance must be an asset for a job like this, Hannah thought and smiled. If any of his clients cut up rough, Mr Vitello looked as though he could deal with it. She held out her hand. "Hannah Weybridge."

He shook her proffered hand, his expression quizzical. "I'm sorry, should I know you?"

By now he had unlocked the office and had opened the door. Hannah activated the hidden recorder and followed him into a cramped room. A desk and four chairs were the only furniture. The walls were covered with shelves weighed down with books, pamphlets and cardboard files.

"I'm a journalist."

"Oh yes. Come to do a bit on community housing?" There was a sneer in his voice that Hannah found intensely irritating. She wondered how effective he was in his job if he always got on the wrong side of people like this, so early in a meeting.

"No, I've come to talk to you about a young woman called Caroline." She held out a photo that had been taken during the interview.

For all of two seconds, Tony Vitello looked disconcerted but covered his discomfort by straightening some files on his desk.

"You knew her a few years ago, I believe?"

Vitello spread his hands and shrugged. "Caroline... now that was a long time ago. I haven't seen her in..."

"You may not be aware that she is missing, even presumed dead following a spate of murders at King's Cross."

"I saw something on the news but I didn't know Princess was involved."

Hannah wanted to jump for joy. Instead she coolly crossed her legs. He'd fallen into her trap. Hannah knew the police had questioned him. And her working name had slipped off his tongue so readily, it suggested he had seen or heard from her more recently than he'd admitted to.

"She's been missing for several weeks and I wondered if she was in hiding and had turned to you for help perhaps?"

Vitello stroked his nose thoughtfully. Hannah glanced at his feet, which betrayed his apparent ease by tapping away on the worn, tiled floor. His shoes looked new and expensive. Just like the boys' trainers in the forecourt. "Why would she do that?" he replied evasively.

"When I interviewed her a month or so ago, she mentioned how you had helped her and that you'd rescued her from two rather violent pimps. She was grateful and spoke highly of you. Maybe she needs protection again?"

Vitello's eyes did not meet her own. Hannah was convinced that he had seen Caroline on the evening she had been working in Streatham. Relief permeated her body as she realised that Caroline hadn't confided the name of the person she was staying with. Tony Vitello had looked totally disinterested when she'd introduced herself.

"I am authorised by *The News* –" Hannah opened her briefcase and brought out the contract – "to pay you for any help and information you might be able to give me…" She allowed the offer to hang in the air between them. Vitello was obviously interested in making a financial deal. "Shall we say £500?" Hannah suggested.

The community worker who looked more Mafioso that a do-gooder was wriggling on the hook. From his clothes and the expensive watch on his wrist, he spent far more than he could possibly earn in this job.

"Shall we say £750 for exclusive rights? That does mean that you cannot speak to or give information to any other media outlet."

Vitello swallowed hard. Easy money… His index finger traced a line from the top of his nose to the corner of his mouth. "Okay. I haven't seen her recently but I'll tell you what I know about her."

Hannah placed her tape-recorder on the table and switched it on at the same time as deactivating her hidden machine.

Hannah left Tony Vitello with little more than she'd started out with. What she was certain of was that, however much of a committed community worker he was by day – and she had her doubts about that – in his free time, he was definitely on the make. If he wasn't exactly running working girls, he was effecting introductions in some way and taking a cut. Probably involved in drugs as well with the kids outside his runners. He spoke so knowingly, he must have had inside knowledge of street life. Hannah wondered again about Gaynor, the lesbian he had introduced Caroline to.

Hannah did not trust him and knew the account of himself he gave apropos Caroline was just a fairy story. She rather hoped some other paper would approach him and he'd blab, thus forfeiting his "fee".

As she walked out of the estate and down the road, she realised she probably wouldn't find a taxi very easily. She stopped to ask a woman if there was a minicab office nearby. She was facing the entrance to the estate and had just learned there was one in the high street when she saw, over the woman's shoulder, Tony Vitello walking out of the Tyneswell.

He looked around, furtively, Hannah thought but it could have been her over-active imagination, and then walked up the road heading north. Hannah thanked the woman and, from the opposite side of the road, followed him. There were enough people about to give her cover and she was intrigued that he should leave his office so soon after returning from lunch. Was his hasty exit prompted by her visit?

Vitello walked fast and Hannah was quite out of breath when she saw him stop suddenly in a side street that, fortunately, boasted a bus stop. Hannah joined the queue and watched in amazement as her quarry roared off in a car he'd just unlocked. Indifferent to cars as she was, even Hannah could identify a Porsche. The number plate said it all: TONY 1

Now what was a relatively poorly paid community worker doing driving around in a car like that? At least he had the grace to park it out of sight of the residents he served. Hannah wished she'd been able to tail him and wondered not for the first time if she should take her driving test again.

TWENTY-EIGHT

"Why can't I babysit for you? I won't do her any harm you know."

"I know that, Caroline." Hannah hoped she sounded conciliatory. "It's just she's used to Nicky looking after her and, to be honest, I'll feel happier."

"Why?" Caroline looked almost ugly in her bad temper.

"Because you're not used to babies, that's why."

"Not good enough, you mean."

"That's not what I mean. Now, the subject is closed. Will you please let me get on and dress?"

Hannah was standing in front of the open wardrobe trying to decide what to wear. The rail was full of things that were unsuitable for one reason or another. *Oh why was everything such a performance. What did it matter what she looked like, for God's sake?*

Just as she was going out of the door, Caroline paused. "Wear that green dress," she advised over her shoulder, "it makes you look sexy."

Hannah didn't turn round. "Well, that's one decision made." *I definitely won't be wearing that one, she thought.*

◊ ◊ ◊

It was a quarter past seven before Tom rang the doorbell. He said nothing about being late. Always punctual to the point of obsession, Hannah was more than a little irritated. She was already on edge about talking to him about Princess and she hated all the subterfuge. She was living two lives and was having trouble making sure neither existence impinged on the other. Except they were inextricably bound.

"Ready?" Tom smiled. He looked... bashful was the word that came to Hannah's mind, although she couldn't for the life of her explain why. Casually dressed in an open-necked shirt, light trousers and jacket, he looked smart, elegant and, Hannah realised with a jolt that brought her up short, incredibly attractive. *Don't be taken in,* she advised herself and the sudden picture of him and Princess together was armour enough.

Hannah collected her bag and jacket and double locked the door behind her. Tom looked puzzled. "What about the babysitter?"

"Oh, I've left Elizabeth at a friend's house." She smiled, then concentrated on putting the keys into her bag. "There aren't that many people I'd entrust her to."

"No, I just thought I heard someone... I must have been mistaken."

But he wasn't mistaken when he saw the curtain in an upstairs window fall back as though someone had been watching their departure. He took Hannah's hand. "What do you fancy? Indian? Chinese? Thai? I didn't think I'd need to book this early in the evening."

They had turned out of Hannah's road and were making their way towards the main shopping street, only minutes away. Living in an area with its broad ethnic and social mix had proved a revelation to her. She had shared flats in smarter areas of London, but East Dulwich was unpretentious and had its own charm. Hannah had been drawn by the relatively cheap housing and nearness to the City.

"The Thai is very good here," she said, thinking how long it had been since she'd been out for dinner. It would have been so nice to imagine that this was an ordinary date with a very pleasant companion. Instead, Hannah had to talk to him yet again about that girl – without giving anything away and in the knowledge that Caroline was in her house and had his ring.

The streets were thronged with people returning from work and early evening strollers lapping up the last of the sunshine. The sun brought a smile to most people's faces and even the tatty shop fronts looked more attractive. It did nothing however to improve the piles of dog excrement which littered the street and which the council cleaners always managed to avoid. Hannah said hello to one or two people she knew and nodded to others.

"Does Elizabeth see her father?" The question literally knocked Hannah off balance as her heel caught in a hole in the pavement and she stumbled against Tom. He held her close, his eyes, it seemed, searching hers. Then he laughed. "Women don't usually throw themselves at me."

"No?" His proximity had shaken Hannah more than the stumble. She could feel herself blushing. Such sophistication. Fortunately, they had reached the restaurant. There were quite a few early diners but plenty of tables free.

When they were sitting facing each other, the meal ordered and a bottle of wine opened, Tom said, "You didn't answer my question."

Hannah was more relaxed. "Who's interviewing whom?" But she smiled at him to take away any implied criticism. "Elizabeth doesn't see her father. He was off the scene before she was born." Hannah ran her finger up the stem of her glass. "We'd been seeing each other on and off for years. He just couldn't face the idea of fatherhood." Hannah looked directly at him. "His loss."

"Yes." Tom looked thoughtful but the first course of satay and fish cakes arrived to distract them.

"I ought to be asking you about Princess," Hannah said after the plates were cleared away.

"Fire away." Tom smiled but Hannah sensed a tension in him.

"Well, to start with, why is there such an interest in a known prostitute leaving an area?"

Tom sighed. "It's not just that she'd left the area, but that the four prostitutes who have been murdered went missing a few weeks before their death and no one seems to know where they were. In fact, it was one of the pimps who first reported one of the girls missing."

"You say girls. Were they all young?"

"Yes." Tom sipped his wine. "They were all young and attractive. Each of them was killed elsewhere and then dumped. Thank you," he said as their main course arrived. "Bon appetit."

They ate in silence for a few minutes.

"Were they all killed in the same way?" Hannah asked.

"No."

Hannah drained her glass. "By the same person?"

"That's classified information."

"But you think there's a connection?"

"I know there's a connection, but I'm not at liberty to tell you how I know this."

"So –" Hannah took a deep breath – "hypothetically speaking, if Princess phoned you to say she was alive and well and living in Scunthorpe, you'd be satisfied?"

"Ye-es." Tom didn't sound convincing. "I don't understand where you're coming from, Hannah. I'm conducting a murder investigation. Four women have been killed. Four women who worked on my patch. I want to find out who killed them and lock them away before they strike again."

"They?"

"Figure of speech."

"Do you think Princess is dead?" Hannah leaned forward, hating the deception and hating Tom for holding out on her. How involved was he? Did he know that Princess had his ring and was that in any way relevant?

"I hope not."

"How well do you know her?" Hannah asked in what she hoped was a disinterested manner.

Tom did not flinch. His blue eyes darkened as they held her brown ones. The moment seemed to go on and on. Hannah was about to repeat the question when Tom reached over and poured some wine for them both. "How well does anyone ever know another person?" he said, then shrugged. "She was a girl working on my turf. I interviewed her a couple of times in connection with crimes committed in the area. She was a nice kid. Streetwise. Sometimes arrogant, sometimes coy, a child lost in a grown-up' world..." Tom sipped his wine.

"Supposing," suggested Hannah, choosing her words carefully, "supposing she knew something and was in hiding, scared for her life?"

"She'd probably have reason to be," Tom said.

Hannah stared at him for a moment. "And how do you fit into all this?"

For a moment he looked confused. "I'm sorry?"

"I was just wondering if murder inquiries are part of a BT Inspector's remit?"

Tom Jordan's eyes narrowed. "You may not have noticed, the city's awash with unsolved crimes. These murders happened on my patch, so I'm investigating them. Of course I report to the Yard. But it suits their purposes to have me front the enquiries. Okay?" His voice was sharp but then he smiled. "Interview over? Let's choose dessert."

Hannah was just tucking into her sankaya when Tom's pager bleeped. He evidently was a man who liked his gadgets. He read the message and smiled ruefully. "My time's nearly up. A squad car is on its way to collect me." Relief and disappointment swept over her in equal proportions. "D'you mind if we skip coffee?"

"No, of course not. Where are you being picked up?"

"Outside your house."

Hannah signalled for the bill but when it arrived and she went to pick it up, Tom laid a hand over hers. "It's all right. I'll get this."

"I'm on expenses from *The News*," Hannah said.

"All the more reason. No one will be able to say I was bought over dinner." He laughed at her expression as he counted out the notes and paid the bill in cash.

Hannah turned in the opposite direction when they left the restaurant. "I must collect Elizabeth," she said by way of explanation.

"Any objection to my coming too?"

"None at all." They fell into step.

"It's strange isn't it? I wish I hadn't met you through *The News* but if it hadn't been for them and Princess, our paths wouldn't have crossed." Hannah didn't say anything. "Why do you write for that rag?"

Hannah sighed. Same old question everyone seemed to ask. Everyone was anti-tabloid these days. "They pay well and I've never been asked to do anything I've found distasteful. You might not like their methods, but they do expose a lot of scandals."

Tom took her hand and turned it over in his. "I wonder," he said almost to himself.

Hannah didn't have time to ask him what he meant as they had arrived at Nicky's. Elizabeth was asleep in her pushchair in the hall.

Hannah hugged Nicky. "Thanks Nicky. Anytime I can return the favour…"

"No problem, I'll speak to you tomorrow." Her goodnight included Tom who seemed perfectly at ease.

They were silent the rest of the way home. Hannah's heart sank at the sight of a panda car outside her home. Oh well it would give the neighbours something to think about. Tom watched her unlock the door and helped her lift the pushchair over the step and into the hall. He bent and kissed her fleetingly on the lips. "I'll call you," was all he said before walking quickly down the path to the awaiting car.

Hannah wondered about the kiss, then smiled to herself. Since Elizabeth's arrival, sex had been the last thing on her mind. "Who needs all that," she told the sleeping infant, "when I've got someone as wonderful as you to love."

TWENTY-NINE

"Are you sure this is the place you want, love?"

Hannah looked out of the window. Number 71 was as derelict as the rest of Tonbridge Street. The boarding covering the ground floor windows had been covered with posters and graffiti. This was King's Cross Women's Centre.

"This is it." Hannah smiled. "How much do I owe you?"

"Seven quid, love."

"Take seven-fifty and may I have a receipt please?"

The driver wrote out the receipt and gave her the change. "I'll hang on a minute until you go in."

"Thanks." Hannah ought to have felt slighted that he didn't feel she was up to looking after herself, but in fact she was amused. London cab drivers were like that. Paternalistic. She turned to wave as she walked up to the unprepossessing entrance and rang the bell.

After a few moments, a woman's voice answered. "Yes?" A dog barked furiously.

Hannah spoke into the entry phone. "It's Hannah Weybridge, I have an appointment with Karen Marshal at 10.30. I'm a bit early."

There was a pause.

"Okay."

A minute or two passed before the door was opened by a young woman wearing black leggings and an outsize T-shirt bearing the legend *Wages for Housework*. The woman had one hand on the door and the other clutched the collar of an enormous German shepherd. The hound growled.

Hannah's smile wavered. She wasn't fond of dogs at the best of times. German shepherds left her distinctly uneasy. She was always worried that they would pick up on her fear.

"Karen?"

"No. She won't be a minute. Come in."

Hannah walked into the grey-carpeted room and the woman and dog disappeared through a door on the other side. Hannah assumed she was to wait where she was; she certainly didn't feel welcome.

She looked about her. From floor to ceiling, the walls were cloaked in posters and notices. The subjects ranged from a campaign against the "SUS" law, police harassment and courts as pimps to *Whores Against Wars* and LAW – Legal Action for Women.

Three black "leatherette" chairs occupied one corner. Two trestle tables were ranged the length of one wall and were piled high with pamphlets and booklets, Hannah was browsing through these when a voice interrupted her.

"Hello, I'm Karen." Black leggings and T-shirt were obviously the order of the day. This one proclaimed *Prostitutes Are Wives & Mothers Too*. Karen's face was devoid of any cosmetic art. Her mousey hair, highlighted blond, was cut short and combed in a no-nonsense fashion off her face. She wore a large, thick-strapped watch, but no other jewellery.

Hannah held out her hand, which was taken in a cool, limp clasp. "Hi, I'm Hannah."

They sat down on the black chairs and Hannah got out her tape recorder. "You know I'm writing a piece for a new women's mag about the pros and cons of legalising prostitution and I just wanted the English Collective of Prostitutes' viewpoint."

Karen regarded her for a moment. "I'm sorry I didn't realise you were going to do the interview now. I thought you were just here to talk about an interview."

Hannah held back the sigh and attempted to keep the exasperation from her voice. She had, in fact, arranged this interview two weeks previously and it had taken several phone calls and reassurances of editorial integrity to get this far. Her copy date was only a few days away now and she didn't have the time or the energy to pussyfoot around. She also wanted to quiz them about the dead prostitutes for *The News* but she wasn't about to reveal that. She had the feeling that any mention of tabloid newspapers would meet with instant hostility.

The smile on Hannah's face felt false. "I have to write this piece over the next few days."

Karen shrugged. "I'm sorry, that's the way the Collective works." She didn't look or sound particularly remorseful.

Journalists were evidently not popular here, so Hannah tried another tack. She bit her lip. "The thing is, Karen, I've had to arrange for someone to look after my baby today… I'm a single parent," Hannah pushed the female solidarity angle, "so it's a bit of a struggle financially and …"

The spokeswoman for the ECP shaped her lips into a smile that didn't reach her eyes. "I'll see what I can do. Wait here."

When she returned after making a hurried phone call that

Hannah couldn't quite hear, she carried a tape-recorder, "Okay, I'll do the interview on condition: we see what you write."

Hannah's heart sank. "That's fine, but you do realise that it won't necessarily be what appears in print. The editor does have final approval."

"That's okay."

"Do you have access to a fax?"

"We've got one here." Karen gave her the number and they both switched on their cassette recorders.

Going home in the taxi, Hannah mulled over the interview. The Collective was highly politicised. She couldn't imagine Princess fitting into that group. They were adamant that prostitutes should not be portrayed as victims. They were women who saw sex as an easy way of making more money for less work. Most were mothers, working to feed their families and keep a roof over their heads. With the recession came an increase of women on the game. Karen did not express any view as to the desirability of this.

The police were seen as totally corrupt. A far cry from Tom's portrayal of the Force. Karen claimed women were victimised, abused, threatened and blackmailed by the law enforcers and when it came to reporting crimes against them, the police just weren't interested.

"One woman," Karen told her, "reported a violent pimp and even gave the police his car registration number. He had threatened to slash her face. And what did the police do?" She stared at Hannah. "They told her to come back when he'd cut her up. They make me spit."

That was about the only personal comment she made. The Collective never revealed which of them were working prostitutes, to protect themselves. Hannah was left wondering about Karen.

But she wasn't left in any doubt about over legalising prostitution. Basically, Karen explained, prostitution itself wasn't illegal, but soliciting, advertising, and women working together, constituting a brothel, were. What the Collective wanted was decriminalisation, not state-run brothels. Hannah had a great deal of sympathy for the cause, having read accounts of how such brothels were run abroad.

When she had asked her about the four murdered women, Karen had given her an odd look, which Hannah hadn't been able to fathom.

"When the first one was found," she said after the briefest pause, "the police were swarming all over the place. Then everything went quiet. Nobody cares about a dead prostitute." She shrugged. "They're making a bit of a fuss now, but maybe that's just because four dead prostitutes make their files look untidy."

Hannah thought about Tom. He hadn't given her that impression. He appeared to care. But maybe for reasons of his own.

"Have the women who work the area any ideas?"

"No." The answer was too ready and brooked no further discussion. As Hannah was leaving she said, "I can arrange for you to interview prostitute women – it's £100 per hour and more for photos."

Hannah gulped. That was a damn sight more than she earned. "I don't think the magazine will stretch to that. We're working to a tight budget."

As the door closed behind her, Hannah smiled. She hadn't liked Karen at all and she was glad she'd made her own arrangements for interviewing some prostitute women.

THIRTY

Hannah walked into the greasy spoon in the corner of Balfe Street. After all the glorious sunshine, the weather had changed. It was a grey, overcast day and the interior actually looked more inviting than it had appeared from the other side of the steamed-up windows. She walked over to the counter and ordered herself a black coffee. In the time it had taken to be poured and paid for, Hannah had made a swift assessment of every female in the room.

Coffee in hand, Hannah made for a corner table. "Mind if I join you?" she asked the woman sitting there reading a paperback: *Felix Holt* by George Eliot.

Dark grey eyes peering over half-moon glasses took her measure. "Suit yourself." She returned to her book.

Hannah sipped her coffee and burned her tongue. "Shit." The woman looked up. Her expression was not inviting. Hannah activated the hidden recorder and cleared her throat. "You're Marti, aren't you?"

The woman's eyes narrowed, but Hannah knew she was right. Caroline, albeit unwittingly, had supplied her with plenty of information. They had watched the documentary programme together – Caroline hadn't seen it previously. Hannah made mental notes as Caroline pointed out landmarks and named cafés and bars they used, giving her very clear clues as to where to find two of the women who had appeared with her in the documentary – although she wouldn't have recognised Marti from the film. In the light of day, she looked older, more tired and very definitely guarded.

"Who's asking?" Her accent was hard to define. There was a Somerset burr underling her hard nasal London tones.

"My name's Hannah Weybridge. I'm a journalist. I interviewed a girl called Princess…"

The woman scraped her chair back. Hannah reached out and caught her arm and in doing so knocked over her coffee. There were some paper serviettes on the table and she mopped up the mess quickly. "Please don't go. I want to help. I'll pay you for your time… I …"

Marti closed her book having carefully inserted a piece of paper to mark the page she was reading. "And just what do you think you can do?"

"I'm writing a piece for *The News* about Princess's disappearance. They're offering a reward for information. Something's got to be done before more women get murdered."

The woman snorted. "More girls you mean. It's only the young, good-looking ones they're after."

"Who?"

Marti looked at her watch. "I've got to go and collect the kids from school." She stood up and walked out. Hannah followed her and fell in step as they walked up the Caledonian Road.

"Did you know the murdered girls well?"

"No."

"Do you have any dealings with someone called Don?" Hannah persisted.

"No I don't!" The woman stopped short. "Look I don't know nothing, right? All I know is that four girls have been killed and nobody seems to be doing much about it."

"Perhaps the article will help... Someone may know where Princess has disappeared to..."

"And what good's that going to do? Fuck all!" Marti looked furious.

Hannah shrugged. "Thanks for your time anyway. If you think of anything, my telephone number's written on this." She handed the woman a £20 note and walked briskly back the way they had come. She was thrown by the encounter. Although she hadn't known what reaction to expect, she had thought that Marti would open up to her. A naïve assumption as it turned out. Or maybe, as Marti claimed, she really didn't know anything.

At the Queen's Head, Hannah drew another blank, Jaynie was not in evidence. She asked the barman if he'd seen her but he said she hadn't been in for a while.

"Try the Mucky Duck round the corner," he suggested, after accepting the proffered £10 note.

Hannah thanked him and left. The Mucky Duck was in fact the White Swan. Hannah ordered a dry white wine; it was so warm, she had to ask for some ice. Jaynie, she discovered, was the young woman sitting smoking gloomily in an alcove.

"What's she drinking?"

"Bacardi and coke?" The barmaid gave her an old-fashioned look,

"Make it a double and have one yourself," Hannah rather enjoyed having the news desk cash.

"Thanks." The barmaid poured the drinks and handed Hannah her change.

Jaynie looked up suspiciously when Hannah joined her with the drinks.

"The barmaid said you were drinking Bacardi," Hannah pushed the drink over to her.

"And who the fuck are you? My fairy fucking godmother?"

"Nothing so glamorous. I'm looking for someone and I thought you might know her." Hannah thought a different tack might be appropriate.

"Oh yeah?" There was no spark of interest. Jaynie's bleached hair was cut short. Her make-up was heavy and not particularly flattering. Hannah thought of how different Caroline looked now. Jaynie must be about the same age.

"I'm looking for a girl named Princess –" the deceit came easier with practice.

"Why?"

"She's missing."

"So?"

"I'm trying to find her."

"Why?" Jaynie gulped her drink. "What's she to you?"

"I interviewed her a month or so ago, for a newspaper."

Jaynie snorted. "We're running a story on her disappearance."

"Big fucking deal." The voice had an affected weariness.

Hannah pulled out some notes. "I can pay you…"

"Lazy bitch!" Hannah hadn't heard the man approach and was stunned as a hand hit Jaynie full in the face.

"What the ...?" Hannah tried to intervene.

"Out." The man's voice brooked no argument, Hannah turned to see a pale, pimply face. The nose looked as though it had been broken several times and there was a long scar running from his earlobe to the corner of his mouth. It made him look as though he had a perpetual smile that was clearly at variance with his usual mood, if now was anything to go by.

Jaynie got up. "I was only 'aving a drink," she said sullenly.

"Outside!"

Hannah swallowed hard as Jaynie moved quickly to avoid another assault.

"And you –" the man turned his attention to Hannah and she tried not to flinch – "you fuck off and leave my woman alone. Right?"

Hannah could only nod. The sheer brutality of the man and the menace in his voice had frightened her more that she cared to admit. She wanted to explain, but decided anything she said would be taken the wrong way and probably make matters worse. She watched him walk unhurriedly out of the bar. The few other drinkers made sure they didn't catch his eye. No one said anything.

Breathing deeply, Hannah concentrated her mind on a mental picture of Elizabeth. When her hand had stopped shaking, she finished her drink and left the bar, aware that at least one pair of eyes was riveted to her movements. In the back of the cab going home, Hannah's composure disintegrated and she gave way to the tears of frustration and anger. She simply wasn't cut out for this type of work.

◊ ◊ ◊

When Hannah got home, there was only one message on the answerphone. Rory's voice came over loud and clear: "Hi, Hannah. Not much joy with the check you asked us to run. We know he moved to the Cross when he said he did but before then seems a bit of a fudge. Stonewalling all round. If we get anything concrete, will fax it over. Take care, won't you."

The message did nothing to allay her fears.

◊ ◊ ◊

As she got into bed that night, her mind replayed the scene in the White Swan. *And the English Collective thinks prostitutes aren't victims,* she said to herself. She wondered if she should tell the girl in the next room, then thought the better of it. Caroline would only tell her what a naïve fool she'd been. *I just don't know anything, do I?* she whispered to the shadows.

THIRTY-ONE

Writing about someone who was missing, even presumed dead, in the sure knowledge that she was very much alive and well and sunbathing in your garden, was proving a difficult task for Hannah. She began her piece several times before she was even remotely happy with it. Facts, she told herself over and over again. Stick with the facts you have been given.

Once or twice she realised she'd written something which implied a deeper knowledge, revealing information she did in fact have but couldn't possibly be expected to know. *Careful,* she admonished herself and felt sick in the pit of her stomach. This was much harder than she'd anticipated. The pink bag was a clue. She'd learned from Caroline that she often left it at the lost property office at the station. She'd dithered about including it, but in the end she did and hoped the subs would delete it as padding.

She read and reread her article, reluctant to let it go. But in the end, there was nothing more she could add – or subtract. The deed was done and she telephoned Rory to say the fax was on its way.

As always when a task was completed, Hannah felt full of energy. She went out into the garden. Caroline was on a lounger. "You're burning. Put some more of this on if you won't cover up."

"Don't nag." Caroline sat up and pushed the sunhat further back on her head. "I don't know, your bathroom's like a chemist's with all those lotions and creams and things. You must spend a fortune."

Hannah laughed. "Not guilty. They're all samples. I write beauty features and get to test the products."

"Nice one." Caroline smoothed more cream on her legs. Hannah watched her. She'd put on a few pounds and, relaxed like this, she looked lovely. What a difference to the beaten-up whore who'd arrived on her doorstep and, thank God, to the photos that were going to appear the day after tomorrow with her article.

"Right." Hannah stood up, "I'm off to collect Elizabeth. Can I interest you in a walk in the park?"

Caroline made a face. "Thought not." Hannah smiled. "See you later."

THIRTY-TWO

Hannah hardly recognised her own article in the double page spread before her. The subs had really gone to town on it. Someone had also managed to get a few good quotes from prostitutes at King's Cross. It made Hannah's sense of failure there even more keen. They hadn't tinkered with Tom's words. Hannah was grateful for small mercies. And mentions of Tony Vitello were fairly tame. The photos of Princess had a very different effect in black and white, somehow more sordid.

The telephone rang, making Hannah jump. "Think it will do any good?" Tom's voice sounded warm and strangely intimate.

"I don't know. I'd like to think so," she said, metaphorically crossing her fingers at the lie. "How are you? I didn't thank you properly for the meal. It was a lovely evening."

"I'm sorry it had to be cut short." Tom's voice was soft. Hannah wondered exactly what he meant and felt herself blushing.

"Yes… perhaps you'd like to come here for a meal some time?"

"I'd be delighted… Just a minute…" Hannah heard him talking to someone else who'd obviously just come into the room. "Sorry

Hannah, something's just come up. I'll have to phone you back. Bye."

◊ ◊ ◊

"There's a cab driver downstairs, sir. He thinks he may have picked up Princess a few weeks ago."

"And no doubt is interested in *The News* reward money?" Tom sighed. This was just the beginning. All sorts would be crawling out of the woodwork at the smell of money.

WPC Spenser shrugged. "It sounds quite promising. He picked up a girl answering to Princess's description in Kentish Town about three to four weeks ago. She'd been badly beaten up."

Tom Jordan tensed. Kentish Town. That tied in with some other information they'd received. This could just be the lead they'd been waiting for. The link they needed. Perhaps Princess had escaped the murderers' clutches. "And?"

"Apparently he didn't realise how badly she'd been injured until he collected his next fare." She paused, guessing what the inspector's reaction would be. "The back seat was covered in blood."

Tom slammed down a file on his desk. "I thought we had an arrangement with these drivers. They're supposed to report anything like that."

Tom turned on WPC Spenser. The anger in his eyes made her take an involuntary step backwards. "I don't know sir, I…"

"And why hasn't he come forward before?"

"He's been away… on holiday… he…"

Tom stopped pacing. "I'm sorry, Avril. I shouldn't be grilling you. I know it's not your fault. It's just we've been working so long in the dark getting nowhere. Then some tabloid rag offers a huge reward for information and hey presto we have a lead. Come on," he said, picking up his jacket, "let's see what he's got to say for himself."

◊ ◊ ◊

The taxi driver, Jim Cole, was in his late 50s; he was thickset with grey hair and a lined face that rarely betrayed his true feelings. He looked as though he might have been a boxer in his youth. He had a paternalistic air. He rarely did stations, he said. And so had slipped the net when the police were interviewing black cab drivers using the King's Cross rank.

"I've been away see… holiday…"

"And why didn't you report the incident before, Jim?"

The driver spread his hands, "Look guv, live and let live I say. She was on the game, right? Got done over? Why should I add to her misery?"

Tom ignored this. "Describe her."

"Well, she didn't look much like them photos. Slim, long blond hair. But she looked a mess. Black eye. Could hardly speak. I did ask her if she wanted an 'ospital but she said no."

"So how did you connect the two?"

Jim was enjoying this and wanted to prolong his moment of triumph. "I didn't at first, did I? When I got the paper last night, I skipped the words an' just looked at the photos. Then later something jolted me. The bracelet she was wearing in the pictures."

"Go on." Tom leaned forward, his whole body tensing.

"Well, I remember noticing it in the street light, didn't I? And the pink bag." Jim paused, knowing he now held their interest.

"Yes?"

"I took 'er back to some street off the Cross and she went into an house and collected this pink bag. Big fluorescent thing it was. She paid me an' asked me to wait. I say ask, it was more like a croak. She could hardly speak, poor cow. Looked like someone had gone for her throat."

Tom and Avril exchanged glances.

"The bag, Jim."

"Yeah. It mentions a pink bag in the paper." He had hoped for more of a reaction, but the two faces before him were deadpan.

"So what happened then, Jim?" Avril spoke for the first time.

"It was a quiet night for fares so I waited, didn't I? She come back and give me a piece of paper with an address on it. Then she slumped in the back of the cab till we got there."

"And you didn't notice all the blood until later?"

Tom swore under his breath at WPC Spenser's intervention. The blood was the last thing he was worried about. He didn't give the driver time to reply.

"Where did you take her, Jim, do you remember?"

"As it 'appens, I do. I log all my fares, don't I. Habit of mine."

"So? Where?"

Jim took out a notebook and made a show of turning back several pages. "East Dulwich."

A jolt that was like an electric shock shot through Tom's body. His mouth was dry. His muscles tensed.

"You don't happen to have the road as well, do you?" he asked with a casualness that would have won him an Academy Award.

"Sorry guv, I only note areas."

"Think back man," Tom commanded but in vain.

"Sorry. Too far back. Been on holiday since then." He smiled. "Still that'll do won't it? For the reward?"

"We'll let you know." Tom stormed out of the room.

It was too much of a coincidence. Hannah Weybridge! That

scheming, lying… He wanted to hit something hard. He had been positive there had been someone else in the house the other evening. He had suspected Elizabeth's father at first, but that was obviously out of the question.

Could it have been the elusive Princess?

Oh Hannah, Hannah…

Why did she have to be involved? And how was she involved? That was something, he determined, he'd know very soon. If Princess had been hiding there…

Back in his office, he picked up his phone then slammed it down again. "No, I'll take her by surprise," he said aloud just as the duty sergeant downstairs buzzed through to him.

THIRTY-THREE

Hannah was sitting at the table, sipping wine and idly shelling pistachios. The wine and sun were having a soporific effect. She felt relaxed. Elizabeth was sitting on a sheet being entertained by a rather boisterous two-year-old.

"Careful, Joel," she admonished as the toddler looked about to hit her daughter over the head with a wooden truck. Elizabeth beamed and made a grab for the vehicle. Their childish giggles filled the air.

On a day like this, it was hard to imagine that evil existed. That Caroline sat imprisoned in her home. Restless. Hannah knew she was straining at the leash. By this time the day after tomorrow, she hoped, Caroline would be gone. The Reverend John Daniels had agreed to have her stay after a brief explanation from Hannah.

Hannah didn't drive, so the vicar was going to meet them at the nearest station. She felt an immense relief and guilt. She wanted to be rid of the girl, but at the same time she experienced a protective, almost maternal, feeling towards her. And then she felt guilty all over again. Her first duty was to Elizabeth. There was no room for Caroline. Literally or emotionally.

The object of her love suddenly shrieked as she keeled over. Hannah picked her up and spoke gently to her, then offered her the bottle. After a few minutes, Elizabeth's eyelids drooped then fluttered open. Clear green eyes stared up at her for a moment, then lost their focus and closed.

"That was well timed," said a heavily pregnant Linda carrying out a tray of food. "We'll be able to eat in peace now. Joel's just given up the struggle to stay awake too. How I'll manage with two of them, I just don't know."

Hannah knew very well. Linda had a talent for organisation that made her well-ordered life appear enviably serene. "You cope with everything," she said with a smile as she placed Elizabeth in her pushchair, which she moved into the shade. "I don't know how you manage it. "

Both Linda and her husband David were teachers in secondary schools. Linda had taken minimum time off to have her first child and would be back at school by the time this child was six weeks old. Hannah wondered how she could bear it.

"With my selfless aid and support of course." David's broad grin robbed his words of any criticism of Hannah's single state. "She'd be nothing without me," he said as he put the barbecued chicken onto the table. "And nor would this meal." He kissed his wife on the top of her head and patted her enlarged abdomen.

Linda gave him a gentle shove. "Go and get some more wine and some mineral water for me. I think the sun's gone to his head," she said to Hannah.

David returned and sat down at the table. "So how does it feel, hitting the big time, Hannah the hack?"

"Ask my bank manager. He's probably happier than I am."

Linda looked at her shrewdly. "This prostitute girl's really got to you hasn't she?"

"Yes and no." Hannah stretched her arms above her head. "It's work. And I have to take what I can get."

"I don't know how you cope with freelance," said Linda as she helped herself to salad. "Always wondering where the next job and fee is coming from."

"Well, I imagine *The News* pays well, doesn't it, Hannah?"

Hannah nodded. "Mmm, this chicken's delicious." She chewed thoughtfully. "It's a bit strange seeing your work sensationalised like that though. I was stunned this morning."

"Ah well, let's hope it does some good and that poor girl turns up alive somewhere." Linda gave Hannah a pat on the arm. "And I think you know more than you're letting on."

"Well, that comes with hob-nobbing with a certain police inspector, I expect," said David. He smiled conspiratorially at Hannah. "Now let's talk about something that's not work or babies."

THIRTY-FOUR

As soon as Hannah walked in, she knew that the house was deserted. There was stillness, a silence that echoed the emptiness. In spite of the sultry heat, which lingered into the evening, a cold tremor ran through her body making her shiver. Elizabeth was asleep in her buggy. Hannah left her in the hall and made straight for the room Caroline occupied.

Everything was extremely tidy. Nothing was out of place, but as Hannah's gaze swept the room, she noticed that nothing was in place either. There was a curious absence of the bits and pieces Caroline left cluttering up the place. No bottles and jars on the chest of drawers. No screwed up tissues smeared with make-up that always looked incongruous set against the background of nursery rhyme wallpaper.

The dark red curtains fluttered in the light evening breeze. Hannah shuddered. In that moment, she knew that Caroline had really gone – presumably forever. Slowly Hannah walked across the room and opened the wardrobe. Empty hangers stared back at her. Hannah wanted to scream. She opened and shut the drawers in a frenzy – they were void of anything that had been Caroline's. The room had not just been emptied, it had been meticulously cleaned. Hannah realised that was what had confused her as she entered the room. It smelled so strongly of cleaning products.

Hannah flopped down onto the bed. For several minutes, her brain refused to take in what her eyes confirmed. She mentally cursed herself. She had known she shouldn't have left her alone today. Today of all days. She should have insisted she came with her to Linda's, but selfishly Hannah had wanted her friends to herself. She had wanted the sort of day she had enjoyed pre-Caroline. A normal relaxing midweek lunch with friends.

Caroline had been very quiet after she had read the article that morning. "You found Tony, then," was her only comment but she looked, momentarily, hurt and vulnerable. For the rest of the morning, she had an absent quality about her and she was very definitely displeased about being shipped off to the Reverend John Daniels. She'd used every argument under the sun to change Hannah's mind. Hannah was deaf to her pleas.

"I need to be in London, Hannah," she wheedled.

"Why?"

"I just do," Caroline replied. She was furious with Hannah. How dare she order her about like this? Like a child. Well she wasn't a child and she wasn't used to having her life run for her. She was pissed off with all the rules. No smoking. No swearing in front of the baby. And precious Elizabeth ruling the roost, her every whim and wish catered for. *Brat!* Caroline sighed. She didn't really think Elizabeth was a brat. She just roused all sorts of feelings in her that she didn't want to think about.

"That's no argument."

"I know." Caroline was worried that Hannah had interviewed Tony. Just when she was getting so near to the bastards who had done for Lisa and the others. But she couldn't tell any of that to Hannah. "I'm a Londoner. I'll be bored rigid in the sticks."

The journalist was unmoved. She had a distinct feeling that Caroline was no longer safe with her. She had no idea what the newspaper appeal would throw up, but it would be better for everyone if Caroline were elsewhere – and protected.

The Reverend John Daniels had asked few questions and Hannah had told him only that she had a young friend who was in need of his protection. He didn't ask what she needed protecting from, nor, Hannah felt, did he want to know. Evil was evil to him, from whatever source. He agreed to have Caroline for a trial two weeks and they could then discuss the matter. Hannah was almost light-headed with relief. This huge responsibility was shifting away from her.

And now she was gone. Though heaven knew where.

"Oh shit!" Hannah's expletive seemed to fill the room. *The ungrateful bitch,* she thought. *Going off and not even leaving a note of farewell.*

A note!

Hannah grabbed the thought like a lifeline. Caroline had probably left a note downstairs.

She had. Propped on the Edwardian mantelpiece in the sitting room was an envelope with her name scrawled across the front. Hannah tore it open. The contents were brief.

Sorry to go off like this but I don't fancy the vicar! Thanks for all your help and thank James too. Don't worry about me. I'll phone soon.

Luv Caroline.

PS You know who's responsible.

It was as though she had been kicked in the stomach by a horse. A physical blow. She read and reread the words: _You know who's responsible._ For the murders was implicit.

Her face was burning. Her stomach churned and she had to make a dash for the loo. Her lunch seemed to have made an incredibly rapid journey through her digestive system. Hannah clutched at the hand-basin for a few moments. In front of her, reflected in the cabinet mirror, a drained haunted face looked back at her. After washing her hands with excessive zeal, Hannah splashed her face with cool water and tried to calm herself with some deep breaths. She put the loo seat down and sat on the edge.

It was preposterous of course. She didn't know anyone who could possibly commit such a crime. Murder. Prostitution. She'd only had a vague idea of that world before _The News_ interview. She remembered two women who worked the pub she frequented as a student. The women seemed then unattractive, sleazy. Part of a different world. One had burst into the loo when she'd been in there. "Don't mind me love," the woman had said as Hannah hovered, rigid with embarrassment. "That bastard! Men are all such bastards…" Hannah had made her exit half apologetically.

And now she'd had a prostitute living in her home, sleeping in the room she'd so lovingly prepared for her baby. And with her had come the whiff of death, disease and deceit. How Hannah hated Princess at that moment. And how she longed to know that Caroline was safe and with someone who would look after her. Not that she was incapable of looking after herself. She had more than proved that. But if there was someone out there, who for some reason wanted her dead…

You _know who's responsible._
I don't, Caroline. I don't!

Hannah's face was cradled in her hands. Her face felt hot and dry. Burning. Her hands were cool.

I don't know anyone who could murder four women, do I? How long, she asked herself, had Peter Sutcliffe gone on leading a "normal" life in front of his friends and colleagues? Not to mention his wife. If she were to be believed. After murderers were convicted, there was always someone who'd creep out of the woodwork and say how strange they'd found the perpetrator, how he'd always acted so differently etc.

Most people were capable of many sins. But murder?

And then she remembered Chris' words: "Of course I could and would kill if I had to." Would kill if I had to... if I had to. Hannah wanted to scream. In that moment she hated Caroline for putting such a thought in her head. For tormenting her.

Another thought flashed into her mind. Caroline had not met Chris. In fact, thought Hannah, as reason reclaimed her mind, Caroline had met remarkably few of her friends. But she had met Gerry Lacon, said a small voice from the recesses of her mind. And Gerry, had been one of her clients, or so she'd said.

Hannah dismissed the idea. He was a doctor committed to saving lives. Or so he had proclaimed. Going with a prostitute wasn't a crime, however unsavoury it might seem. And yet all the dead women were prostitutes... Hannah thought of Sarah. Surely she would know. No. Maybe it had been a case of mistaken identity. Caroline had mistaken Gerry for someone else. After all, a lot of her business was done in half-light.

You know who's responsible.

Responsible. That was the key word. Someone she knew – and Caroline knew – was involved, not necessarily the murderer. Someone who had dealings with prostitutes.

Tom Jordan!

For a moment Hannah couldn't breathe. *Please God, don't let it be him.* It mustn't be him. It must not. She liked Tom. There was something very attractive about him. And then she recalled the ring.

Caroline had Tom's ring in her possession. He said he'd lost it, but was he telling the truth? And was Caroline? Hannah decided that when the girl rang, she'd ask her to explain everything. At least she'd know and not be wracked by these unpalatable possibilities.

Elizabeth stirred and murmured as she picked her up, carried her upstairs and placed her in the cot. Hannah gazed down at her sleeping child and felt that overpowering love surge through her veins.

"I love you, darling," she whispered.

She watched the tiny mouth make little sucking movements and heard a deep sigh escape her daughter's lips. Hannah smiled and tiptoed out of the room.

She went into what she now thought of as Caroline's room and looked round. Everything was just the same. Hannah felt the tears well up. "I've let her down."

For a few minutes, Hannah gave way to her emotions. Then, making an effort to pull herself together, she blew her nose and came to a decision. When Caroline rang, she'd invite her back – to stay at least until they could work out an alternative that was acceptable to Caroline. No more Reverend John Daniels. Hannah made a mental note to phone him early the next morning just as, on cue, the telephone rang.

Hannah went into the study to take the call.

"Hannah?"

"Yes."

"You okay? You sound a bit nasally."

"Touch of hay fever, I think."

"Hmm." There was a brief pause. "Look I'm phoning from the hospital. I just picked up a patient's copy of *The News* and – well – I – um – it's her isn't it?" James's voice had actually risen a pitch.

"James, please don't ask me anything. She's gone and I don't know where I –" Hannah's voice broke.

"Oh Christ, Look I'm first on call. I can't leave but I'll be with you as soon as I can tomorrow. Okay?"

"Okay. Oh and James – "

"Yes?"

"Will you bring that package we sent you?"

"Sure. Oh there goes my bleep. I'll see you tomorrow."

THIRTY-FIVE

Hannah slept fitfully.

At three o'clock in the morning, she got up to make herself a cup of hot chocolate and wandered from the kitchen to the sitting room. She switched on a lamp and her eye caught her copy of *The News*. She picked it up and settled on the settee.

Her "Princess" story was spread over pages two and three with a teaser on the front page. Hannah opened the paper and saw that Caroline had drawn spectacles on her photos. There were a few more doodles but nothing which might act as a clue.

Hannah sat drinking her chocolate and wondering where Caroline had gone. And with whom? Hannah cursed herself for not challenging the girl with the knowledge that Tony Vitello was living in Streatham. What was it Tom had called him? A nasty piece of work? Well her own observation confirmed that. But more to the point, did Caroline trust him? Had she trusted him?

Hannah dipped her finger into the chocolate froth. She felt something, some vital clue was eluding her. She picked up the note she'd left on the coffee table and looked at it again, studying Caroline's childlike handwriting. It was the postscript that caught her attention. It really did look like an afterthought. As though it had been written hurriedly.

Something that had been niggling at the back of her mind suddenly leapt forward with startling clarity. Supposing Caroline hadn't left of her own volition?

The more Hannah thought about it the more it seemed likely. The note was a decoy. Written to allay any fears. And the postscript a pointer, maybe a warning for Hannah herself to be careful.

On the other hand, there had been no indication of a struggle, of any violence. But did there have to be? Hannah asked herself. Perhaps Caroline had answered the door innocently enough and then had been persuaded by some means – a gun? – to depart quietly leaving a note to quell any suspicion? And the cleaning up – it was as though Caroline had never been there…

Hannah shivered from both the coolness of the early morning and the fear, which was taking root in her mind. If Caroline had been forced to leave, then she was obviously in grave danger.

Taking the cup into the kitchen, Hannah tried to make some sense of it all. The worst-case scenario was that whoever had tried to kill her, had somehow discovered that Caroline was still alive and had tracked her down. Presumably to make sure they did a proper job this time. Hannah took this appalling thought back to bed with her.

As she slipped under the duvet, Hannah realised with searing clarity how close she and Elizabeth had come to being snared in the same net. If they had been at home too… the prospect didn't bear thinking about. Unless… unless whoever it was had been watching the house and had waited for her and the baby to leave. Or else someone had acted out of consideration for her. Someone like Tom Jordan? Hannah felt sick and weary and more alone that she'd ever felt in her life.

◊ ◊ ◊

Shortly after ten, the phone rang. Elizabeth was safely ensconced with Nicky and Hannah was sitting at her desk staring at a blank screen and trying to focus on teenage marriage. Her next assignment.

Hannah rested her hand on the receiver. She didn't want to pick it up but equally she did want to know if Caroline was on the other end of the line.

"Hannah Weybridge."

"Hannah, hi it's Rory. You won't believe this but we've had a lead on Princess's disappearance."

"Really?" Hannah tried to sound enthusiastic but her heart was plummeting.

"Yeah, some cab driver remembered picking her up. Took her to your neck of the woods, actually."

"Oh." The blood drained from her body. Or that was what it felt like. Her arms were leaden. Her skin prickled. She knew there was a question she had to ask. "Do the police know?"

"He went there first. Was interviewed by your inspector yesterday morning."

Hannah tried to swallow the bile that was threatening to choke her. Could Tom really have come up with the – hopefully, to him – unlikely possibility that Hannah had been shielding Princess all the time? Had the taxi driver remembered the address? Doubtful. Unless there had been some reason for him not to forget. And she wasn't the only person living in East Dulwich. But Caroline was gone and Tom… Tom …

"Hannah? You still there?"

"Sorry Rory, I was just wondering. Have the police followed it up?"

"I don't know. They sounded a bit cagey this morning. But that's probably because they're feeling a bit miffed."

"Why?"

Rory laughed. "Oh you know. All those weeks of detective work bearing no result, then we lure out a witness with great rewards. Must be galling."

"Yes."

"Well –" Rory wondered at the monosyllabic answers. She could show a bit more interest. "Thanks for all your help. I'll be in touch."

Hannah shook herself. "Thanks Rory, it's really kind of you to let me know so quickly. You feel a bit out of it working from home. Thanks."

"Right. See you."

Hannah wondered if she would. Unlikely.

◊ ◊ ◊

For a long time after the call, Hannah sat at her desk, head in hands. How much did Tom Jordan now know? Was it safe to call him? If she hadn't been hiding Caroline, she would have called him, delighted he'd got a lead. But she wasn't that good an actor.

And Caroline had left her warning.

You know who's responsible.

Hannah had already had her suspicions about the inspector, which Caroline would neither confirm nor deny. But she did have his ring! That was something Hannah couldn't dismiss.

If she didn't phone him, would he wonder why? Hannah scratched her hand. She knew she didn't have the strength for such subterfuge that conversation would demand. She was close to breaking point. Better to wait. Do nothing.

◊ ◊ ◊

At lunchtime, Hannah took herself off to Nicky's.

"You look dreadful," Nicky greeted her. "Worse, if anything than this morning."

Hannah shrugged.

"Anything I can do?"

Hannah dredged up a smile. "You've done more than enough, stepping in for me with Elizabeth. I don't know what I'd have done without you."

"Hmm." Nicky followed her into the sitting room. Elizabeth and Liam were sitting in the playpen. The baby girl stretched up her arms, wearing the special smile she reserved for her mother.

Hannah breathed in her daughter's fragrance. Elizabeth grasped at her hair and chuckled. Hannah felt the knots around her heart tighten and she wanted to weep – for the joy of Elizabeth and the agony of the loss of Caroline. She cleaved the infant to her and kissed her head, her chubby fingers and her soft cheeks. This was what was important. She had done nothing wrong other than to omit to tell a police officer that a certain person he was worried about was in fact living in her house.

THIRTY-SIX

Tony Vitello brushed his shoes in time to the song he was humming tunelessly to himself. Satisfied with the result, he donned his jacket and quietly slipped out of the flat. His phone call had worked amazingly quickly.

It had been surprisingly simple to get through to the man at home. He was actually listed in the directory. A piece of luck that bode well for him. He was going to be a very rich man.

He walked jauntily around the corner to the side road where he had parked his Porsche. He didn't notice two men disengage themselves from a small group who were sitting on the steps of a large house opposite, drinking beer from cans. Beer that the two men had so thoughtfully provided when they unobtrusively joined the group listening to the England versus the West Indies test match coverage on the radio.

They caught up with him just as he was unlocking the car door.

"Mr Vitello? Tony Vitello?"

His body tensed for combat as he swung round. His martial arts training was no match for the hypodermic needle, which plunged into his side. Within seconds, his lifeless body slid down the car. His face held an expression of surprise. The two men slipped away before his body hit the ground.

◊ ◊ ◊

The message light on the answerphone flashed three times.

"Hannah, James. I'm just going into theatre. A pump job so I don't know what time I'll be back. May be late. I'll ring again before I leave the hospital. Bye."

"Tom Jordan here. I'm rather tied up so don't ring back. I'll call again soon."

"Hannah, hi it's Cheryl Thompson. Just wondered when we could expect the teen marriage piece? Speak to you soon. Bye."

The one voice Hannah wanted to hear above all the others was absent. *Oh Caroline where are you?* She rang Cheryl, who was in a meeting, and left a message that the feature would be with her within the next two days.

And then she stared at the still blank screen. Inspiration was in short supply but, Hannah told herself, so was money. She couldn't afford the luxury of worrying about Caroline. She needed money to support Elizabeth. And there was absolutely no point in having someone else looking after her baby daughter while she mooned around.

For the next two hours, Hannah concentrated with a supreme effort of will. Finally, she sat back in her chair with a passable first draft before her. She sighed and stretched her arms up high, allowing her head to loll backwards. Hannah missed the exercise classes she used to attend before the advent of Elizabeth. You could really work off stress then. She was never disciplined enough to exercise on her own.

She longed for a sauna and a Jacuzzi, but immediately thought of the compensatory small body, which nestled into hers in the small hours of the morning. She was so proud of Elizabeth and of herself for having borne her. And yet it is such an everyday occurrence. Women have babies. They become mothers for better or worse. Hannah hoped she would always be the mother Elizabeth needed. Not like Caroline's mother.

It occurred to her that she'd never asked Caroline her surname. She wondered if Tom knew. Had he, in fact, visited the mother in the unlikely event of her daughter finding sanctuary there? Apart from sending her money, did Caroline keep in touch with her mother?

Certainly with me she doesn't, thought Hannah, cursing the girl yet again for not phoning. *I don't care where you are so long as you are safe. And if I don't hear from you by tonight, I'm going to read the photocopy of your notebooks.*

The ringing phone made her jump.

"Hello, Hannah Weybridge."

Silence. No, not silence, Hannah could hear background noises. A typewriter? Muffled voices. The line went dead. Hannah fervently hoped that someone wasn't checking her movements. *Don't be so paranoid,* she told herself. But she couldn't prevent the knot of fear lodging in her stomach. She switched on the answerphone and went to collect Elizabeth.

She didn't notice the man leaning against the van opposite her house, reading a newspaper.

DANCERS IN THE WIND

THIRTY-SEVEN

The television was on for the early evening news.

Elizabeth and Liam were playing happily on the floor. Hannah smiled as Nicky came in carrying two glasses of white wine.

"Lovely, just what I need." Hannah sipped gratefully and turned her head slightly towards to television as the newscaster said:

"A man was discovered dead by the side of his car in Streatham, South London, this afternoon. He has not been officially identified but local people named him as Tony Vitello, a local community worker. Mr Vitello lived nearby. Police are treating the circumstances of his death as suspicious and appeal for witnesses to come forward…"

Hannah had turned white. Her eyes looked enormous, the shadows under them deeper. Nicky touched her hand, which was icy. "Hannah… Hannah… what on earth …?"

"I… I… excuse me I …" Hannah's head rolled back onto the top of the Chesterfield and her eyes closed.

Nicky's light touch on her arm brought her back to the present. Hannah turned to her and smiled wanly.

"Sorry I've just had a bit of a shock, that's all."

"Did you know that man?"

Hannah shook her head. "No." She reached for her wine and drank deeply. "No, not really. But I interviewed him the other day about that missing prostitute. I just hope it's not connected in any way."

"What do you mean?" Nicky was intrigued. She knew little of Hannah's work world, but was witness to the obvious strain she'd been under the last few weeks. And, she was willing to bet, it had nothing or little to do with being a single parent. Hannah was hardly the stereotypical deserted woman.

"Well, his talking to *The News* and then his murder."

"If it was murder." Nicky squeezed her hand. "But whatever the cause, it's not your fault. You didn't kill him."

"No?" Hannah forced a smile. "Maybe it's just a horrible coincidence. God, I'll be glad when this is all over."

"All what is over?" Nicky had a shrewd idea that Hannah was more involved than she let on, but they didn't know each other well enough for real confidences yet.

Hannah contemplated the other woman. It would be so nice to get it all off her chest but… "The investigation," she said obliquely. She picked up Elizabeth. "Now I think we'd better be off, don't you, little one?" Two pools of green looked up at her. Hannah lifted her so their faces were level. They rubbed noses. Elizabeth's chubby arms reached out. Dimpled fingers clutched at her hair. "Come on, you bully."

"How are you fixed for tomorrow?" Nicky asked at the door.

"Could you possibly have her for the morning? I only need a couple more hours' work on the article."

"Fine. See you about nine then."

Hannah kissed her cheek. "Thanks, Nicky," she whispered and Nicky was left wondering what exactly was going on.

◊ ◊ ◊

Before bathing Elizabeth, Hannah checked the answerphone. One voice needed no introduction.

"Hannah, I wanted to catch you before you hear the news. Tony Vitello is dead. Not my patch of course, but it looks suspicious. We're waiting for the post mortem. We need to talk. I'll phone you later. Take care."

James's disembodied voice followed. "Sorry Hannah, I won't be back tonight – another emergency. I'll speak to you as soon as I can. Be careful." The last words seemed to be underlined.

Hannah went downstairs and locked and chained the door. Then she went through to the kitchen and made sure the garden door was bolted. She had always felt so safe in this house. Being alone had never bothered her before. Should it now? If only she knew who the enemy was – for sure. She needed to read Caroline's notebooks and could do nothing before then. Unless, of course, Caroline phoned. That possibility seemed more and more remote.

Hannah bathed Elizabeth, and once she was asleep in her cot, ran a deep bath for herself.

From the other side of the road, a man watched the house from the vantage point of his white transit van. He spoke into a radio-phone.

"Party is now at home. Property was inspected before her return."

◊ ◊ ◊

She was in the bath and didn't hear the front door open and close. Facing away from the door, the first she knew of the intruder was a ghostly presence reflected in the steamed-up mirror opposite her. Her eyes widened momentarily as the chloroform on the gag hit the spot and she sank under the bubbles, lifeless.

Within minutes, her body had been lifted, the bath cleaned, and various items removed. Outside, a private ambulance waited, but no one was particularly interested as the front door opened and two paramedics wheeled out a body on a stretcher. Seconds later they and Princess were gone.

THIRTY-EIGHT

Hannah felt no better after her bath. Her mind kept returning to Tony Vitello's death. It was obviously murder, but was it because he had talked to her? That was hardly likely, seeing as he'd said so little and offered no new information on Princess. And she was missing too. Hannah dismissed the idea that Caroline was involved.

And what about Tom Jordan's role in all this? Hannah was glad that she hadn't had to speak to him in person; she'd be sure to give herself away. *Oh Caroline why did you have to pick on me? And why haven't you phoned?*

The ringing broke into her thoughts. Hannah stared at the phone on her desk. Innate caution made her switch on the answerphone. She heard her own voice apologise for being unavailable and ask the caller to leave a message.

There was a pause. "Hello?" said a hesitant voice unused to leaving messages on machines. "It's Marti here. I ..."

Hannah snatched up the phone. "Hello Marti, it's Hannah."

"Oh it's you I... well anyway. I thought we'd better have a chat.

I'm in the White Swan. Can you meet me here?"

"Ye-es. When?" Hannah's pulse was racing.

"Tonight."

"Well I – "

"Look, I can't hang around, I've got a punter. Wait for me if I'm not here." The line went dead.

Hannah made two calls. One to Nicky whose husband was home and she was prepared to come round and babysit. The second to book a mini-cab. Hannah dressed quickly in cotton trousers and a large T-shirt and fitted the tiny recorder she still had into her bra.

The minicab and Nicky arrived at the same time, so there was fortunately no time to explain her hasty departure. "I'll be back as soon as I can," she promised on her way out through the front door. "Oh and lock the door behind me."

◊ ◊ ◊

The White Swan was not as busy as it had been earlier in the evening with commuters grabbing a pint before catching their trains, but the regulars made quite a crowd. Hannah looked round but couldn't see Marti through the haze of cigarette smoke. She made her way to the bar.

"Hello luv, back again." A statement rather than a question from the barmaid she'd bought a drink for. "Not looking for Jaynie again, are you?"

"No, why?"

"'Er bloke's not someone to cross." She leaned forward over the counter and lowered her voice. "An' the old bill's taking an interest. Bloke by the dartboard."

Hannah waited a moment before turning slightly. She looked over straight into the piercing gaze of a man she vaguely recognised.

For a moment she couldn't place him, then she remembered he'd been in the pub when she'd met Jaynie. "What's his name?" Hannah asked under cover of ordering a spritzer.

The barmaid measured the wine into a glass and stood directly in front of Hannah as she added the soda. "Don Martin," she said in a low voice. "And mine's Mary," she added with a smile.

"Hannah. Have one yourself."

"Ta very much." Mary turned away to get Hannah's change.

Just as the latter was sipping her wine, a man's voice startled her. He was so close, she could feel his breath on her ear and could smell the acrid odour of stale sweat, beer and cigarettes.

"You doing business luv?"

Hannah swung round to the florid face of a man in his 40s, just an inch or two taller than herself. His fine, wispy hair was heroically trying to disguise a receding hairline. Froth from his beer outlined his full, flabby lips and there was no way his stubble could be called designer. A black T-shirt, straining over a large beer gut, which made him look about seven months pregnant, failed to meet his jeans, which looked as unsavoury as their wearer.

"I'm sorry?" Hannah instinctively leaned away from him.

"I said, are you doing the business?"

Hannah's throat went dry. She felt disgust, pity, fear in equal quantities. She was almost mesmerised by the horror the man presented. She opened her mouth, but the words she heard came from a different direction.

"No she isn't, Dave, and you can piss off," Mary hissed as she handed Hannah the change.

"My mistake, no offence meant." Dave shrugged and moved away to be swallowed up by a group of drinkers at the other end of the bar.

As Hannah watched his departure, she realised the whole scene had been taken in by the officer at the dartboard. His face was unreadable, but Hannah's gut feeling was that he had put the other man up to it. But what on earth for? Just to embarrass her?

"You wanna watch him."

"Who? Dave?"

"No, him –" a slight movement of her head indicated the policeman. "'E's a shit of the first order. Be careful." And with that eloquent warning, she went off to serve someone else.

A raucous belly laugh erupted from the other end of the bar and Hannah felt as if all eyes in the pub were on her, mocking her. The atmosphere seemed friendly enough, but there was an undercurrent of menace that Hannah did not like. *God, these women earn their money,* she thought. And she wondered how Marti, with her taste for classical literature, coped. How did any of them, she mused.

"Mine's a large Bloody Mary, luv."

Hannah's reflections were interrupted by the arrival of Marti who was hardly recognisable in her working garb. A long, lightweight yellow plastic raincoat covered a black micro skirt and camisole top. Her legs, emanating from high boots, were bare and bronzed. Her face was heavily made up.

"Don't you get hot in all that?" Hannah asked as they took their drinks over to a free table in the corner.

Marti shrugged. "It's practical," was all she said. She took two gulps from her glass.

"Have you seen Princess?" Hannah asked, knowing what the answer would be but praying for a miracle.

Marti shook her head. "Princess isn't the only one missing you know?"

Hannah, worried about saying anything that might put off the other woman, remained silent. She had already turned on the concealed recorder.

"I know of two other girls who haven't been seen for a few weeks." Marti lit a cigarette and inhaled deeply. "Someone is recruiting the young ones, offering a lot of dosh to work somewhere. And I don't think it's your common or garden brothel either."

She tilted her face upwards as she blew out a long stream of cigarette smoke. "I'm not even going to look at that shit by the dartboard –" involuntarily Hannah gazed in that direction. Don Martin was draining his pint. "But he's the one to watch."

Her words echoed those of the barmaid.

"He's got his crooked little finger in it somewhere. And I bet he's not the only one at the nick either."

Hannah must have looked incredulous. Marti sighed. "You've got a lot to learn, luv. He actually runs a couple of girls – well as good as. The maggot. If he doesn't know where those girls are, I'll…"

"Night off, Marti? Pedro must be going soft in his old age." Don Martin placed his empty glass on their table and made for the door. His words conveyed a warning that Marti was quick to pick up.

'Bastard," she muttered as she stood up.

Hannah looked confused. Marti had got her here to talk and now she was leaving.

"It was nice meeting you again, Hannah." She held out her hand and as the other woman clasped it, she felt a piece of paper being pushed between her fingers. "Good luck."

Hannah slipped the folded paper into her handbag.

◊ ◊ ◊

It was dark outside and much cooler now. She paused for a moment by the entrance to get her bearings. Not many cabs came down this back street. The place looked deserted.

The street lamps were out and there were no lights coming from the closed shops and offices. Hannah thought about going back into the pub and ringing for a minicab. But that would mean waiting and she was desperate to get away from the place. The station was only a few minutes' walk away and it would be easy to get a taxi from there. She set off at a brisk pace.

The steel was cold against her throat. A hand was clamped against her mouth in such a way that it was impossible for her to breathe. She tried to swallow the bile that rose in her throat, but as she did so, the tip of the knife sank into the soft flesh under her chin. Her right arm was yanked further up her back and a muffled moan of pain escaped her.

"Quiet, bitch!"

The voice came from behind her right ear. "I've got a message for you see –" the hand forced her head backwards and the blade scratched the surface of her skin – "you've bin arskin' too many bloody questions. Upsettin' people you are. An' it's no good fer yer 'ealth. Got it?"

The knife pressed harder against her flesh. She tried to nod, but couldn't move. She made a deliberate effort to relax her body. The adrenalin was pumping through her. Now. She stepped back onto her assailant's foot and, as the man pulled back creating a space between their bodies, she elbowed him in the groin with all the force her left arm could muster.

"Fucking bitch!"

The knee came up and sent her flying, face forwards onto the pavement. The kick that followed was ill-aimed and lost most of its impact before it made contact with her recumbent form.

"Fucking bitch! You've been warned."

As she turned her face, she saw a dark shape disappearing into the darker shadows. She leaned forward and threw up. Slowly she stood up and brushed herself down. She took a few breaths and wiped her mouth with a tissue. She could smell and taste the blood and vomit. But she was still in one piece. And she still had the piece of paper Marti had given her.

During the taxi ride home, Hannah had tried to make some sense of what had happened. She had talked to Tony Vitello and now he was dead. Marti had been seen talking to her. Would she be safe? As to her own attack, it all seemed rather amateurish now. Somebody must have been paid to frighten her off. But it could have been so much worse. Maybe they – whoever they might be – thought she would scare easily. But it only served to strengthen her determination to find out what had happened to Caroline and the missing girls.

The taxi's running engine sounded grotesquely loud in the somnolent street as Hannah paid the driver and asked him to wait.

"Hannah! What's happened to you?" Nicky looked appalled.

"Nothing, it's okay. I'll tell you all about it tomorrow. There's a taxi waiting out there to take you home. It's paid for."

Nicky looked about to protest but seeing Hannah's mutinous

DANCERS IN THE WIND

expression decided against it. "Okay I'll see you tomorrow."

Hannah hugged her. "Thanks for looking after Elizabeth at such short notice, I... I... I'll explain everything as soon as I can."

Nicky nodded and was gone. Hannah locked and bolted the door then dragged herself upstairs to the bathroom. In the harsh light, she could see a little blood had congealed on her neck and the beginnings of a bruise on her jaw. Otherwise she just looked dirty. Nothing a shower and some antiseptic wouldn't cure. How to cope with the terror that now invaded her was another matter.

As soon as Nicky had gone and she'd locked the door, she'd taken out the piece of paper Marti had given her. In neat italic script was written *Gillespie Clinic, Harley Street* followed by the names of four very prominent men. Hannah read and reread the names. No wonder Caroline had been scared that no one would believe her.

Caroline was running towards her. Hannah could see her mouth moving but couldn't hear what she was saying. There was so much noise. Voices of people she couldn't see properly. Try as she might, she could not make out the words Caroline seemed more and more desperate to convey. Hannah was rooted to the spot. She couldn't reach her. Her own voice was lost in the mists. Suddenly there was sobbing, sobbing...

Hannah sat up. Her body was drenched in sweat. For a moment she couldn't think where she was or what was happening. Then the wakening world assumed control. Elizabeth was hollering. Hannah glanced at the luminous figures on the clock/radio and groaned. Three in the morning.

Reluctantly she swung her legs out of bed. Her feet met the

carpet and in two steps she was beside the cot and comforting the infant. The room was airless. With Elizabeth in one arm, she opened the small top window – something she normally avoided because of the car fumes in the morning. As she did so, she noticed the white transit van. It had been there earlier in the evening. Not a usual parked vehicle in this road. For a brief moment it occurred to Hannah that she was being watched. It was difficult to dismiss the idea as pure paranoia after what had taken place only a few hours previously.

"Oh Elizabeth, what have I got into?" Hannah took the baby back to bed with her, still haunted by the dream of Caroline and the attack.

THIRTY-NINE

"What gets me about all this. Sir…" Alan Doveton began as he entered the inspector's office bearing coffee and a bacon sandwich.

"Thanks, Alan." The smell of bacon made his mouth water. Hunger had left him in a ratty mood. "So what gets you?" he asked wearily.

"Well sir, when the first body was discovered, the boys from the Met were swarming all over the place." Doveton moved his weight from one foot to the other.

"Ye-es," Jordan encouraged between mouthfuls.

"Then suddenly there was a news blackout and you were left more or less in charge."

"And you don't think I'm up to the job?" Tom quipped, but Doveton was aware of the underlying edge in his tone.

"No sir…" He caught sight of Jordan's raised eyebrow. "I mean, yes sir. What I mean is …" Alan paused for effect "… you must admit it's a bit unusual."

"The Yard's still involved. They're just keeping a low profile."

"But why, sir? I don't like it. It's like someone's going to end up with egg on their face and they're anxious it's not them."

"Interesting." Tom eyed him speculatively. Doveton looked about to say more but changed his mind. "By the way, sir, Don Martin hasn't reported in and he's not answering his phone at home."

"No, he wouldn't be." Tom Jordan looked grim. "He was arrested by Special Branch last night."

Doveton's face was a picture of incredulity. "What the hell for?"

"Well. If running a couple of prostitutes isn't enough for you, how does arranging for a woman journalist to be beaten up grab you?" Tom took another bite of his sandwich and chewed thoughtfully as he watched Doveton's expression, which would have been comical, if he hadn't been so concerned about Hannah.

"I trust," he said with quiet authority, "there are no other officers in my squad whose extra-curricular activities warrant such attention?"

Doveton was spared an answer by Avril's appearance at the door.

"There's a call from someone who calls himself Snapper on line three sir.

Tom smiled. "Thanks, Avril, I'll take it in here."

Two minutes later, he was agreeing to meet one of his best informants – Snapper. It seemed he had a car registration number for sale.

◊ ◊ ◊

Inspector Jordan made his way to the lost property office in the station. It was where Sam Smith, also known as Snapper, worked and it wouldn't have been unusual to see a policeman in the vicinity.

The office seemed deserted, but Tom saw the electric kettle had just boiled, steam still filtering up the spout. Two huge mugs of strong tea stood on the tray. Tom picked one up, then winced as the hot liquid burned his tongue.

"How's business, Sam?"

Sam had shuffled into the room. He was tall and lean and was younger than the shock of grey hair first led you to assume. He grinned, perching himself on the edge of a stool. Childhood polio had left him with a distinct limp in his right leg. Now in his late 30s, he was the eyes and ears of the terminus. He knew every wino, dope dealer and whore. Especially the whores. One or two did him for free, or so Tom had heard. Sam had taken the deaths almost personally.

"You know squire, umbrellas an' walking sticks a speciality. Mind you –" he sipped his tea – "we 'ad a right to do in 'ere yesterday. Some MP left his briefcase on the train. Full of top secret papers or something. Anyway it turned up again intact."

While he had been talking, he passed Tom a scrap of paper with a car registration number written on it. Tom folded the paper and slipped it into his trouser pocket. The tea was still hot but he drank it down.

"That's the car that… that car picked up the girls." Sam pointed to Tom's pocket. He blinked rapidly and blew his nose loudly. "I liked that little tart…"

Tom gripped his shoulder. "Thanks, Sam." He replaced his mug on the tray together with a folded £20 note and left quickly.

FORTY

Hannah was sitting on the settee with her legs curled up under her. She looked haggard and so did James who had just driven over after a 72-hour shift at the Hammersmith. Hannah made a large pot of coffee that was standing, ignored, on the table between them.

"Where's Elizabeth?"

"She's with Nicky today. She's stepped into the breech while I find a new nanny."

James leaned forward and filled two mugs. No milk, no sugar.

"So."

Hannah ran her fingers through her hair. "I haven't done anything illegal you know."

"No? Why were the police looking for Caroline, Princess or whatever else she calls herself?"

"She calls herself Princess. Her working name. I insisted she use her real name for protection."

"From what?"

Hannah shrugged. "She told me she'd been beaten up by two

pimps because she wouldn't work for them. Obviously there's more to it than that." Hannah hadn't decided how much she should confide in James. His whole demeanour shrieked disapproval and she wasn't that much of a masochist.

"So why didn't she go to the police?"

"She… she seemed to think that they were involved in some sort of cover-up. Even when Tom Jordan contacted me …"

"Who's he?" James interrupted. "And how on earth do you know this girl in the first place?"

Hannah topped up their coffees and then told him about the initial interviews she'd done with Princess and Tom. By the time she'd finished, she felt as though she'd been through a wringer. James didn't look much better.

"So you think the answer may lie in this package?"

"I'm sure it does." If Hannah hadn't felt so tired and irritable herself, she might have been amused at the way James held onto the envelope in such a possessive way.

"Supposing I just had it over to the police?"

Hannah couldn't believe what she was hearing. Was he serious? After everything she had just told him? If Tom was involved in some way – well there was bound to be a cover-up and she could endanger Caroline's life.

"James, I …"

"Don't worry, I won't. To be perfectly honest, I really don't want to get involved. Obviously, if I have to, I'll confirm the injuries she had sustained when she arrived here but …"

James handed her the envelope. "Do you want me to stay while you go through this?" If he read the mute appeal in her eyes, she read the exhaustion in his.

Hannah looked down at the envelope then at James. "Could you sleep here?" She looked embarrassed. "I know it's an imposition but I'd feel happier with someone in the house with me and I won't disturb you. I…"

James grinned. "Just direct me to the bed. By the way," he said as they went upstairs, "how did you come about that bruise?"

"Caught it on a cupboard," Hannah replied, slightly appalled at how easily lies came to her these days. She was glad James had his back to her.

Hannah leafed through the photocopied sheets until she recognised the date of her dinner party when Caroline had acted so strangely. She read the entry:

I nearly shit myself! It's him, the fucker! And there he is with his wife all sweetness and fucking light. I didn't know what to do. Panic! I forgot about my hair and glasses. I was sure he'd clock me. But when Hannah introduced us, he just shook hands and then turned away as though I wasn't worth his interest…

I sat where I was. I don't think I could have moved if I'd wanted to. Earlier Hannah had said just keep quiet and look bored if I felt awkward.

Awkward! I was going hot and cold. My throat was so tight I couldn't even drink my wine. That man makes my flesh crawl. Harley Street doctor! Harley Street pimp more like. He's always on the lookout for girls for his fucking sex therapy clinic. Some clinic. More like a torture chamber. He had a special room for S & M. Only the thing was it was the girls who got beaten. Usually whores get paid a fair sum to whip the shit out of some fancy bloke. There, well…

Lots of girls were tempted. It was good money. It had to be. Though the chances are you wouldn't be in a fit state to spend it. There was a rumour that one girl disappeared from that place. She was certainly never seen again. Not on the beat. Someone got carried away. Someone murdered her. And then Lisa. After what happened to me I know she was murdered....

Strange that they didn't take the money back when they dumped me...

I don't like being hurt, being hit. And I recognised him. Do you know me, young lady? He asked in that posh, plummy voice they all have. I shook my head. I'm not that stupid. I played dumb but even I know Robert Bowldon's face.

Hannah stopped reading. Robert Bowldon had held several jobs in Government. Currently he was the Home Secretary's right hand man. No wonder Caroline didn't want to go to the police. They were answerable to him.

Somehow she wasn't shocked that Gerry Lacon was involved. Maybe it was just a relief that so far Tom Jordan's name hadn't been mentioned. She read on.

He couldn't get it up. Then he hit me. He kept hitting me and not just with his fists, objects. Then I saw he's got a hard on. He rammed it in me. He kept pushing until I was screaming out and then I felt his fingers round me neck. I tried to pull them off. It just got him more excited and then I must have blacked out...

Tears were pouring down Hannah's cheeks. Poor, poor Princess. She blew her nose noisily, not sure that she could take in very much more. What she had read so far had sickened her. She found it hard to believe that apparently sophisticated men could be so depraved. But Caroline's description, together with Marti's note, made sense of all the imponderables.

Christ, this was a time bomb waiting to explode in the face of the establishment. She wondered how many other prominent men were involved. Not that they were all necessarily killers but…

◊ ◊ ◊

By the time James woke up, Hannah was sitting at her desk fingers flying over the keyboard. She almost wished she had a typewriter so that she would have had the satisfaction of pounding the keys to get rid of some of the aggression, the rage she felt inside.

James stood in the doorway, watching her. She became aware of his presence and turned to him.

"Hi. Feeling better?"

"Yep, but not for long. I've just been bleeped."

"What do they want to do? Kill you?"

James shrugged, resigned. One day he'd be a consultant and would be able to choose his hours.

"So what did you find out?" James noticed her heightened colour.

"Nothing very savoury." She reached over for the envelope. "I made some more copies while you were asleep. Would you mind holding onto one for me?"

"Look, Hannah, about the police…"

"I'm going to the police. James. I'm going to hand over a photocopy and let them read it for themselves."

"Well, that's a relief."

"And I'm going to *The News* with the story."

"What?" James's face was a study in disbelief.

"I am a journalist, you know."

"But not in this league, Hannah." He could almost feel and taste the antagonism that remark provoked. "Don't get involved in case it all backfires on you," he said more gently.

"I am involved, James. And Caroline's life is at stake."

James wasn't impressed. "Isn't there someone closer to home that you should be concerned about?"

"That was uncalled for! What a low –"

"Ok I'm sorry. Look I've got to go. I'll take this with me."

He leaned over and kissed the top of her head. "Life's a bitch isn't it? I'll call you. And for God's sake be careful, Hannah."

FORTY-ONE

Hannah was still writing when the bell rang. She wasn't expecting anyone. She breathed deeply to calm herself. Fear seemed to be her constant companion these days.

The bell rang again.

She padded silently down the stairs and looked through the spyhole. Tom Jordan.

Hannah opened the door. The inspector looked almost as haggard as James had done.

"Hello." He summoned up a smile.

Hannah returned his smile and stood aside for him to come in. "Have you got anything to drink?"

Hannah was taken back by his request and his manner. *Humour him,* she thought.

"There's some whiskey in the kitchen, top cupboard on your left."

Tom went straight there, found the bottle and poured a generous measure. Hannah noticed there was only one glass. He walked back into the sitting room. "Where's Elizabeth?"

Everyone seemed to be concerned for her daughter. "She's with Nicky…"

"Good."

For an awful moment, Hannah thought he was about to kill her and was glad the baby wasn't there. Then he put his arm around her shoulders and led her to the sofa. Hannah was dumbstruck. She looked into those blue eyes that held hers and tried to fathom their depths.

"Princess is dead." His grip tightened on her shoulder. His eyes never for one second left hers. "Her body was discovered this morning on some waste ground behind the station."

Hannah thought she was going to faint. Her eyelids felt heavy. She tried to say something, but no words came out. Her body slumped against Tom's and he held her even more closely for a moment.

"Here, drink some of this." The whiskey had been for her.

Hannah drank. The spirit burned her throat and she coughed. The moment of faintness had passed. She looked at Tom. He looked so trustworthy, so –

"I… I …" she couldn't get the words out.

Tom came to her rescue. "I know she was staying here," he said quietly holding a finger to her lips as she attempted to say something. "Don't say anything now. We can talk later. In fact, I'll have to interview you – later."

His arm had not left her shoulder. She was drawing strength from him. He was being so kind, so understanding when he had every right to be furious with her if he was on the level. If he had known Caroline was with her, then …?

"I wanted to tell you myself. I didn't want you to hear it on the news or through your newspaper friends."

Princess is dead. Princess is dead. It's over. They've won.

Slowly, Hannah pulled away from him and walked unsteadily out of the room. She returned with a bulky envelope.

"I was going to give this to you today, anyway." She handed him the package.

He looked at it and then Hannah.

"It's a photocopy of Caroline's – Princess's – notebooks. She wrote everything down. You'll find what you need in there. Names…"

The sob rose in her throat and tears gushed down her distraught face. "And… and … just in case there's any kind of cover-up, *The News* also has a copy." They didn't – yet. It was just a piece of insurance for Hannah.

Tom was standing before her. She found herself within the powerful circle of his arms. "Oh Hannah, Hannah," he said, then kissed her hair gently. Tears were soaking his shirt but he didn't move away. Hannah clung to him. Gradually the sobs ceased wracking her body and she pulled away from him.

"And last night I was attacked."

Tom nodded. He knew. She felt icy. How the hell did he know that? She hadn't reported the incident. "And it seems one of your men is…"

"He was arrested last night by Special Branch. He paid someone to put the frighteners on you."

Hannah's eyes widened. She couldn't suppress the shiver that ran though her body. Tom put his arm once more around her shoulder.

"Come on, I'll take you round to Nicky's."

Yes, that was what she needed more than anything. To be with her child.

Tom locked the door for her as Hannah noticed the police car with a WPC at the wheel. Good. A witness. Then her gaze travelled across the road to where the white transit van with its blackened windows was still parked.

Tom directed Avril to Nicky's home. He took her to the door.

"I'll have to speak to you officially and I'll ring you later." He smiled at her.

Was that the smile of a guilty man?

It was only much later that Hannah wondered how Tom had known about her attack. Had Special Branch been tailing Don Martin or had she herself led them to him? If so, how long had they been monitoring her movements?

FORTY-TWO

Her heels echoed on the tiled floor. Each step in time with her pulse, which pounded in her ears. The corridor was cool, chilly even, but the shiver that ran through her body had nothing to do with temperature.

"Sorry, Hannah," Tom had said on the phone. "I hate to ask you to do this but officially you were the last person to see Princess alive and her parents haven't seen her in years. Even the other working women hadn't seen her new look."

Hannah had agreed to identify Caroline's body and a squad car had collected her and taken her to the morgue.

Avril Spenser had smiled sympathetically. Dead bodies. She remembered her own reaction to seeing Lisa. Her stomach had heaved, and to her utmost mortification, she'd vomited in front of her colleagues. Not to mention DI Jordan.

They reached the glass panelling that covered the top half of the left hand wall. Avril touched Hannah's arm. Silence. No sounds from the world outside intruded. Someone brought the trolley to the window.

"Are you ready?"

Hannah nodded, unable to speak.

The attendant on the other side lifted the cover to reveal the face of a young woman. Hannah hadn't known what to expect, remembering the way she had appeared when she had collapsed on her doorstep all those weeks ago. She'd hardly recognised her then.

Now the auburn hair had been combed back from her face, which bore no sign of violence. She looked as though she could have been sleeping deeply.

"Yes, that's her."

Avril nodded to the attendant and steered Hannah back down the corridor. Again, the echo of her heels. And round and round in her head swam the words: "I failed her." She was unaware of her tears until Avril passed her a bunch of tissues.

They walked out into the bright sunshine. Back into the living world where Caroline would never again walk. Hannah stumbled. Drained of energy, her legs almost gave way.

"Sit here for a moment." Avril guided her to a low wall and sat alongside her.

Suddenly she realised that this was tough for the WPC as well.

"I'm so sorry."

"Don't apologise." Avril blew her nose noisily. "Think you can make it to the car now?"

Hannah stood up. "Yes, thank you."

During the journey back, both women kept their own counsel. Hannah had put on her sunglasses and Avril had the impression she'd closed her eyes but obviously wasn't dozing. The officer drove on in silence. At one point, her car radio spat into life and she switch it off. Whatever was happening could wait. Neither of them needed reminding of the darker side of life and death.

The car came to a halt just a little up from Hannah's house. "Would you like me to come in with you?"

"Would you mind?" Hannah felt a complete wimp.

"Not at all. I need the loo anyway." Avril locked the car after them and followed Hannah to her door. She noticed that the locks had been replaced. Hannah dropped the keys as she went from the mortice to the Yale. Avril retrieved them and opened the door. The two women looked at each other before going in but for very different reasons.

Hannah held on to Elizabeth long after she had fallen asleep. Suddenly her leg jerked and she was wide-awake. It was after midnight. Hannah's exhaustion had overcome her. She walked upstairs and placed the baby in the cot.

As she went to draw the curtains, she noticed that the rear doors of the transit van were open and someone was getting in. She stood where she was, unable to look or move away. The doors shut then opened and the same – or another? – shadowy figure got out and walked swiftly up the road.

Hannah stood there her arms folded in front of her chest. Each hand clutching the other upper arm. She should have told Tom about the van. But perhaps he knew all about that too. Hannah closed the curtains. Tom hadn't phoned her and she was desperate to know what he thought of Caroline's accusations. His silence didn't bode well.

She went to the bathroom and ran a deep bath, throwing in the first thing she laid her hands on. The fragrance was lily of the valley. Lily of the valley, she loved that little flower. The bubbles covered her, caressed her body... and her mind drifted back to another scene in her bathroom. Herself washing Princess. Washing away the blood and make-up. Patting her bruised and swollen body dry. Applying ointments and creams. Easing her into an old dressing-gown.

Hannah felt hot tears course down her scalding cheeks, making little rivulets that ended their journey in the now-cool bath water. Better get out. She dried herself quickly and slipped into bed, convinced she wouldn't be able to sleep. Her eyes closed almost immediately and she didn't wake again until five in the morning.

Knowing she needed to be active, to be doing something, Hannah got up and went to her study. The screen was still green. She hadn't turned off the computer when Tom arrived. Hannah read what she had written and then in silent agony changed the first two paragraphs. Princess was no longer missing. She was dead.

The printer was still grinding on when Elizabeth woke.

"Rory? Hannah Weybridge here."

"Hi Hannah, how're doing?" He didn't wait for an answer. His tone changed slightly. "I don't know if you've heard but Princess has turned up – dead."

"Yes I know. It's about that I –" Hannah's throat constricted and she made herself swallow hard.

"You all right, Hannah?" Rory couldn't cope with tears. He was making frantic signs to the secretary to come over but she had a more engrossing engagement with her nail file.

Hannah coughed, took a deep breath and tried to keep her voice pitched lower. It sounded more businesslike.

"I have an exclusive on her death. I'd like to come in and discuss it with you."

Maybe Rory hadn't heard her correctly. "Do you want to fax over the details?"

"No, I don't." Assertive, not aggressive she told herself under her breath. "I'd like to come in and see you and the editor."

"Well we do have a planning meeting today and ..." Rory was trying to stall her.

"What I have is an exclusive about the murders of four – sorry five – prostitutes and I can name names. If you're not in the market for the story, I'll go elsewhere."

Rory digested this information. Hannah sounded as if she meant business. Sod the editor's wrath if she didn't come up with the goods. You have to take risks sometimes. "We do have a meeting, Hannah, but get in as soon as you can and interrupt us. We'll be waiting for you."

◊ ◊ ◊

Hannah had chosen her clothes with care. She needed to look the part and if she couldn't interest *The News* with the story, she'd have to try the other nationals. Her cream linen suit still just about fitted her and the low-heeled green shoes matched the silk shirt, which had been one of her more successful impulse buys. As a boost to her confidence, she sprayed herself liberally with a sample of Caroline Herrera she'd been sent. The face that looked back at her from the mirror didn't look too bad considering how she felt. Concealer to cover the shadows under her eyes and a bit of blusher had worked wonders. She didn't want to confront them looking as though she was about to burst into tears.

The toot from the mini-cab told her it was outside and she collected her handbag and briefcase, took one last look at herself in the hall mirror and put her head round the sitting room door. It was a habit she'd fallen into but, of course, Caroline wasn't there. She never would be again.

FORTY-THREE

"Christ, this is dynamite," Rory looked up from Hannah's typescript and echoed her own first impressions when she read Caroline's notebooks. She'd brought in two copies of her own account for good measure. The editor was reading the other.

Hannah knew Georgina Henderson by repute but she'd never met her. She was slimmer than she had looked when she appeared on numerous television chat shows, her features sharper. The suit she was wearing was Armani, her shoes, Gucci. Her jewellery looked absolutely the real thing and her ash-bond hair, cut fashionably short, and make-up were immaculate. Hannah felt like the poor relation next to her. Incongruously, Georgina's nails were bitten to the quick, making her fingers look short and stubby. Hannah looked at her own neatly manicured fingertips and felt marginally better.

"And you say," said Georgina – everyone in the office called her George but never to her face – "that you have the notebooks?"

"I have a photocopy," Hannah corrected her.

"And how did you come to have it?"

"Caroline, that is Princess –" Hannah knew this was going to be a sticky point – "gave them to me."

"I see." Ms Henderson referred back to the pages in front of her. "And she's been staying with you?" Hannah was about to make some sort of answer, but Georgina suddenly smiled. "What a brave lady."

Hannah didn't know if she was talking about herself or Caroline.

"This is, as Rory so succinctly put it, dynamite, Hannah." The editor's fingers drummed lightly on the desktop. There was something in her tone that Hannah found irritating. "And we will have to make our own investigations but –" suspicious, there was something suspect in all this but Hannah was too innocent in the ways of tabloid editors to work out exactly what was bothering her.

Then she dismissed the thought as Georgina buzzed the phone on her desk. "Get me Larry Jefferson up here will you, Mandy?"

She gazed at Hannah, considering. "For really big stories like this we get our lawyer in to draw up a special contract," she explained with a smile, which looked too practiced. "It won't take long. Why don't you take Hannah over the road for a drink, Rory?"

It was their dismissal.

When Hannah returned to the office, Georgina was waiting with a four-page contract. "Read it at your leisure," the editor said casually. "Basically, it states that we agree to pay you the sum of £17,000 –" she heard Hannah's slight intake of breath and knew she'd gauged her correctly – "for exclusive rights to this story. You can talk to no other papers or media until we have published…"

Hannah wasn't really listening any more. £17,000! £17,000.

What did strike her as odd was that they gave her a cheque there and then and advised her to pay it in right away. Thinking of her overdraft, Hannah was only too happy to comply.

It was only in the taxi going home after a detour to the bank that the hard truth hit her. £17,000 was poor compensation for Caroline's death. She wasn't going to benefit. Blood money. It really was blood money. Hannah felt disgusted that she was actually benefitting financially from Caroline's death. With just enough time to ask the driver to pull over, she opened the door and vomited into the kerb-side.

◊ ◊ ◊

When she got back to the house, having collected Elizabeth, there was a message on the answerphone asking her to ring Tom Jordan as soon as possible.

"I need your statement, Hannah." He sounded oddly constrained. "I'll send a squad car over to pick you up."

It sounded like an offer she couldn't refuse.

"Ok, but I'll have to bring Elizabeth with me, I've only just got her home."

"No problem." At last she could hear a smile in his voice. "See you soon." He rang off.

◊ ◊ ◊

Hannah strapped Elizabeth into her car seat and carried her out to the waiting car. It was the same woman officer as before. Hannah noticed one or two curtains twitching and guessed she'd be invited into a few neighbours' homes for coffee or a drink over the next couple of days. She smiled at Avril.

DANCERS IN THE WIND

"I'll sit in the back with the baby if you don't mind?"

"Go ahead." Avril returned the smile and wondered if the rumours that were circulating the office about their esteemed boss and the lady journalist were true. He certainly seemed concerned about her. Well, good for him, she thought as she eased the car into gear and glanced at the mother and child in the rear view mirror.

◊ ◊ ◊

"Right, if you would just initial each sheet and then sign the final page, that will be it."

Hannah smiled. The interview had been remarkably easy. Too easy. Hannah almost had the impression that they were humouring her, though she couldn't think why. Elizabeth had gurgled happily throughout the entire proceedings.

"I'll run Ms Weybridge home."

Avril, who had sat in on the interview, and Hannah looked at each other.

"I'm off duty now."

So it was true, thought Avril gleefully.

Oh no, thought Hannah, her heart sinking. Now he would really grill her.

FORTY-FOUR

"I still can't understand why you didn't tell me." Tom was driving fast, but skillfully. The roads were busy but not yet clogged with early evening rush hour traffic. "Why didn't you trust me?"

"I promised Caroline. And she thought that with the type of people involved – well, that the police wouldn't exactly be on her side." Plus, she thought some officers were involved. Certainly one was.

Tom grunted. "I hope nobody is above the law," he said, but it was without conviction. He knew in his bones that there would be a cover-up. Someone would go down for the murders, but not the real killers – of that he was sure. Unless… unless *The News* came up trumps. And then, where would that leave him?

He pulled up at the red lights and stared at Hannah until she felt herself blushing under his scrutiny.

"There's something else, isn't there?"

The lights changed.

"Isn't there, Hannah?" he asked quietly.

"I don't know," she answered. And she didn't. She didn't know if she could broach the subject of his ring. *Did he find it with Caroline's possessions,* she wondered?

She was still wondering when she became aware that they had stopped outside her front door.

"That white van," Hannah began.

"Is one of ours."

Hannah stared at him, wide-eyed and incredulous.

"This is a very nasty business, Hannah. It's there for your own protection. Just to make sure you don't have any unwelcome visitors."

The revelation made Hannah even more uncomfortable. Who or what was the "ours" referred to? Surely BT Police didn't have that sort of surveillance gear. *Special Branch?* she asked herself as she carried Elizabeth into the house.

"There's a beer in the fridge if you'd like one," she said.

"Thanks. Look, Hannah, we do need to talk."

Hannah looked up into his face. Her pallor spoke volumes. "Not now Tom, please. I can't take any more. I just want to have a shower and put on some fresh clothes. I…"

"Okay, okay." Tom grinned his boyish grin. "How about you take a shower and I entertain this young lady?" He swung Elizabeth into the air, sending her into peals of giggles.

"It certainly sounds a good idea." Hannah left them to it. She was amazed that Elizabeth didn't protest. She usually made such a fuss when Hannah left the room these days.

◊ ◊ ◊

As she stood under the shower, letting the jets of cool water blast away some of the tension in her body, the image of Tom swinging Elizabeth into the air stayed with her. Hannah wondered how

Elizabeth would feel about not having a father. Would she blame Hannah? Would she feel deprived of masculine company and dash out and marry the first unsuitable man who showed her some tenderness? Hannah snorted. Time enough for those thoughts.

◊ ◊ ◊

When she went downstairs, wearing an old but comfortable cotton dress, the cigarette smoke from the pub she'd been in with Rory washed from her hair, Hannah felt more able to face Tom and his inevitable, awkward questions.

Then came the sudden awareness that the house was quiet. Ominously quiet. For one heart-stopping moment she thought Tom had run off with the baby. The events of the last few days had had an alarming effect on her imagination.

She swallowed hard and pushed open the sitting room door, stopping short at the sight before her. Tom was slouched in an armchair, Elizabeth in his arms. Both bodies absolutely motionless. Deadly still. It was several seconds before Hannah realised they were both sound asleep.

Her first reaction was to remove Elizabeth, but as she stood watching them, one small blond head tucked comfortably under a stubbly chin, one tiny hand clutching a reassuring thumb, they seemed so at peace she didn't want to rouse them. Tom certainly looked as though he needed some sleep.

Smiling to herself, Hannah tiptoed out of the room. There was something she had to do and now was probably as good a time as any. She braced herself and walked into what she had come to consider as Caroline's room. She had no need of a bed now. Sadness threatened to engulf her until she looked at the nursery rhyme figures on the wallpaper. This was Elizabeth's room and needed to be so again.

Hannah removed the bedding and started to roll up the futon. The wooden base was strutted and as she pulled it into its upright position, something, or rather two things caught her eye.

The leather-bound picture frame was lying face down on the carpet. A strange place to leave it, thought Hannah as she picked it up and stared into the youthful face of a man dressed in an army uniform. He bore a remarkable resemblance to Caroline.

And I didn't believe her when she did tell me the truth, reflected Hannah sadly.

She put the frame to one side and then reached over to retrieve the other object whose hiding place she had disturbed.

It was Tom's ring.

She stared at it as it rested in the palm of her hand. Now why had Caroline left this and the photo? Had she hidden them on the day she left – or some time before? What did it mean?

One thing it means, Hannah told herself, *is that you'll have to give it back to Tom.* His reaction would be interesting, she reflected numbly. And more important than she cared to admit even to herself.

FORTY-FIVE

Tom stared down at the ring Hannah had handed to him with a terse: "Yours, I think." There was no mistaking the signet ring; the insignia was so distinctive.

"Where on earth did you find this?" Tom looked totally bewildered.

"You'd be surprised," Hannah mumbled almost to herself.

She searched Tom's face for some clue in his expression. He looked amazed but not in any way embarrassed as she thought he would be. In fact, he had a slightly dazed air about him, which was partly due to the fact that he had not long woken up to find Elizabeth still slumbering in his arms, her mother watching him speculatively from the other armchair.

"You said you'd lost it." Hannah's tone was nothing if not accusatory.

Tom ran his fingers through his hair and shook his head. He must be missing something here. "I did lose it."

"Where?"

They stared at each other. Their eyes locked, the tension between them almost palpable.

"Does it matter where?" he asked, his calm tone deceptive.

"Yes it does."

"Would you mind telling me why?" A muscle in Tom's jaw was working overtime. She was almost mesmerised by the agitated movement.

"Because of where I found it." Hannah's heart was pounding. Although she stood her ground, she mentally cursed herself for confronting him like this. Elizabeth sleeping on the sofa afforded no safeguard. If he turned nasty now there was little she could do to protect herself.

Tom saw the fear in her eyes and bit back what he was about to say. *Sit down.* He told himself. The last thing he wanted to do was intimidate her. He sank into the armchair and leaned forward, elbows resting on his knees.

"I lost my ring on duty one evening," he said quietly. "I was arresting a dope pusher who suddenly turned violent and in the scuffle that ensued my ring must have slipped off." He spread his hands and met her eyes. "I went back and searched the area the next day but there was no sign of it." He smiled. "So how do you come to have it?"

Hannah sighed. This was going to be worse than she imagined. "Caroline –Princess – left it here."

The silence hung heavily between them. Tom was the first to speak. "How?"

Hannah misunderstood him. "It was hidden under her bed."

"No, how did she have it? Did she find it?" He shrugged. It was hardly important now. Or so he thought.

"She told me she had been given it – by a punter." The last word seemed to have been dragged from her.

It was several seconds before Tom realised what Hannah meant. "You surely don't think I gave it to her?" Hannah's expression confirmed that that was exactly what she thought.

"Oh come on. What do you take me for?" Tom stood up. "Jesus, Hannah!" He wiped his hands over his face, then knelt in front of the silent woman and gently took both her hands in his.

"Let's get this straight. I am not and never have been a –" he looked as though even using the word with reference to himself was a trial – "a punter. I have never had sex with a prostitute and don't intend to. I would have thought," he said looking into her face and willing her to believe him, "that you would have known that much about me by now."

Hannah bit her lip.

"And, equally importantly, I would never have given this ring to anyone. It was my father's. He died a few years ago. He remarried after my mother died and we didn't see so much of each other. I regret that deeply." He swallowed hard and Hannah watched his Adam's apple rise and fall. "It's the only thing of his I had."

Tom stood up and pulled Hannah to her feet. He wrapped his arms around her and sighed into her hair. "Is that why you couldn't trust me?"

Hannah nodded into his chest.

"Oh, Hannah. You didn't think I was involved in all this mess?" His tone was resigned. He felt gutted.

"I didn't know what to think," she said with a sob and he stroked her hair as once again she soaked the front of his shirt with hot, salty tears.

When she raised her face, his lips brushed hers but there was a faraway look in his eyes and a tightness about his expression.

"I think I'd better go."

Hannah searched his face for a clue to what he was really

thinking. *I'd be furious if I were him,* she thought. She moved away from him, took a tissue from the box on the coffee table and blew her nose.

"I'm sorry." She couldn't think of anything else to say. She willed him to go quickly, at the same time wanting desperately for him to stay. They stood across the room from each other. Tom was the first to look away.

"I'll be in touch," he said in a way that made Hannah think that would be an unlikely event. "And, Hannah – "

"Yes?" She almost held her breath.

"For God's sake, be careful!" In two strides, he was out of the room and she heard the front door close after him.

Hannah collapsed onto the settee. Totally drained, sickened and, it had to be said, more afraid than she'd ever been in her life.

FORTY-SIX

For two days Hannah heard from neither Tom Jordan nor Rory at The News. She watched and listened to every news bulletin she could. There was nothing new on the prostitute murder hunt. In fact, it was suspiciously absent from the media.

At last, she took matters into her own hands and rang Rory.

"News desk."

"Rory?"

"Yup?"

"Hannah Weybridge."

"Right." A pause. "Could I ring you back?"

"Er – yes." Hannah was surprised by his tone. She was even more surprised when, ten minutes later, her phone rang.

"It's Rory. Look I'm sorry about that but I couldn't speak from the office." It sounded as though he was ringing from a pub. "To put not too fine a point on it, your story's been spiked…"

"What!" Hannah was thunderstruck.

"It was vetoed from upstairs." Upstairs was the euphemism for the proprietor, Lord Gyles. "George is in on it too, I think, but I can't be sure. All I know is that the copy has disappeared and I've been told in no uncertain terms to forget I ever saw it. The whole thing stinks."

"But, but they can't do this!" Hannah struggled to control her voice. "They paid me all that money."

"A drop in the ocean to that lot, darling. Look, I must get back to my desk. Sorry about your story. I'll let you know if there are any developments. Ciao."

Hannah carefully replaced the received. So it was happening. The cover-up. Everyone closing ranks. Well, she'd see about that. She'd take the story elsewhere.

Hannah dialed again. "Georgina Henderson, please."

"Who's calling?"

When Hannah gave her name, she thought she heard a change of tone in the voice. "I'll just see if Ms Henderson is available." The secretary's voice was replaced for several minutes with insidious music. "I'm sorry, Ms Henderson is in conference at present. Can I take a message?"

"Yes, I'd like to speak to her about a story I submitted. Perhaps she'd call me back?"

"Does she have your number?" Hannah would love to have rung the officiousness from that voice.

"She does."

"I'll see she gets the message." The line went dead.

Hannah cursed. If Georgina Henderson rang back, she'd eat her hat. But the phone did ring 20 minutes later making her nearly jump out of her skin.

"Ms Weybridge?"

"Yes."

"Larry Jefferson here." He paused as if waiting for recognition. "We met at *The News* the other day."

"Ye-es." If she had thought about it, she wouldn't have been surprised to hear from *The News'* lawyer.

"Ms Henderson asked me to ring you…"

Hannah decided a direct approach was the best policy. "My story's been spiked, Mr Jefferson and I'd like to take it elsewhere."

"I'm afraid that's impossible, Ms Weybridge."

"I will, of course, return the money."

"Ms Weybridge… Hannah, did you read the contract?"

Hannah hated his supercilious tone. "Yes, I…"

"It states quite clearly that *The News* owns the copyright. You accepted the payment. It is not your story, Hannah. We own it outright."

"I'll rewrite it for another newspaper," Hannah threatened.

"Then we'll have to take out an injunction against you. Until *The News* publishes the story, you are under contract not to talk or write about the subject."

"But it's been spiked."

"Exactly, and so are you Ms Weybridge. Good day to you."

◊ ◊ ◊

Hannah phoned John Abrahams, a solicitor she knew. He asked her to fax the contract to him and got straight back to her. *The News* was totally within their rights and there was, it seemed, nothing Hannah could do.

Hannah strapped Elizabeth into the pushchair. "We're going on a nice long walk around the park," she told the infant as she adjusted the sunshade. "Mummy needs to walk and think."

Elizabeth clapped and gurgled loudly.

Dulwich Park was about 20 minutes' walk away. Hannah and Elizabeth arrived there in just over ten. Fury drove Hannah on at speed. As she went through the tall iron gates, she slowed down and willed herself to think, calmly and rationally.

She never thought to look behind her. If she had, she would have seen she had been followed. Her pursuer was hot and red-faced and spoke into a small radio before entering the park after her.

FORTY-FIVE

After lunch, Elizabeth had her nap and Hannah sat down to compose one of the hardest letters she'd ever have to write. It took several drafts, but eventually she was reasonably satisfied with the result.

Dear Mr Collins,

You don't know me but your daughter Caroline spent the last few weeks of her life at my home. I know you must be extremely distressed by her tragic death, as I am.

I am returning the photograph she kept of you on the back of which I found your address which I also gave to the police, so they will have contacted you by now. Caroline was a lovely, brave girl who didn't deserve her fate. And she loved and was inordinately proud of you.

She told me that the reason she never contacted you was that she didn't want you to see what she had happened to her. I hope, therefore, you will be able to remember the daughter she was, not the stranger she had become.

After much deliberation I have decided to send you a copy of Caroline's notebooks. It will not make easy or pleasant reading for you and I think you should consider long and hard before you open the enclosed envelope.

I have tried to expose your daughter's murderers through the press. However, they have closed ranks to protect the guilty. You may have access to people who may be able to help. I don't know.

I hope you have someone there to bring you comfort in your grief. Yours sincerely,

Hannah Weybridge.

Hannah stared at herself in the mirror. The image reflected had a haunted air. She was sure she could also see a few grey hairs. Her skin looked tired and dehydrated. Her eyes dull. With dark shadows beneath them. Small wonder.

Some beauty writer eh? The laugh was hollow and the woman in the mirror did not look amused. *Some news reporter too!*

Hannah stripped off and gave herself the sort of treatment she wrote about in women's mags. Salt rub, deep cleansing, mud body wrap, shower and more showers – the works. Throughout it all, she gave vent to her emotions, allowing her tears to mix freely with whatever she happened to be applying.

The physical cleanse made her feel marginally better. Elizabeth's demanding company helped. She had to go on doing everyday things. Feeding, cleaning, changing and, above all, loving. Elizabeth made life bearable. But what sort of world had she bought her daughter into? And were they safe?

That evening, Hannah swallowed her pride and rang Tom Jordan. He was at home but he didn't sound at all friendly.

"I'm sorry I can't talk now." He sounded abrupt to the point of rudeness.

Hannah was thrown of balance. "I just…"

"I'm on my way out, Hannah.

"Oh, sorry."

"I'll speak to you soon.

"Yes, bye." She spoke to the dialing tone. Hannah hung up, deflated and defeated. She had been astonished by her attraction to Tom. It had been a pleasant surprise. She had thought that motherhood had wiped out all such feelings from her. But Tom managed to fan the flames a little. And he had liked her. Past tense was appropriate, Hannah thought. She picked up a novel she was reading but couldn't concentrate. She turned on the television. Some mindless game show was suddenly interrupted by a news flash.

A grim-faced Martyn Lewis appeared on the screen.

"Good evening. News has just come in that Robert Bowldon, minister at the Home Office, died an hour ago at the Westminster hospital. His car exploded in the car park of the Houses of Parliament. No one has yet claimed responsibility. We'll bring you more news as it comes in. And, of course, there will be a full report in the nine o'clock news."

His face faded and was replaced by the games show.

Hannah turned off the television. Was it just a coincidence? Was Robert Bowldon's death, so soon after her revelations to the police and *The News*, a quirk of fate? She felt bewildered, frightened and sickened.

Who was responsible, and if they were anything to do with Caroline's death, was she also in their sights? Her thoughts turned to Tony Vitello's sudden death. How did he fit into all this, apart from having known Caroline? Whose side had he been on?

The ring on the doorbell had her stomach somersaulting. Her hands felt clammy, her body leaden as she walked into the hall and peered through the spyhole. At first she couldn't make out who was standing in the half-light.

"Who is it?" she called, willing her voice not to betray her fear.

"It's Tom, Hannah."

Hannah unchained and unlocked the door.

"You're the last person I expected," she said and then realised there was another man standing behind him. Her eyes widened and she actually felt faint.

"Can we come in please?" Hannah's body was blocking the doorway. She nodded and stood aside as the two men entered. She noticed the younger man was carrying a black leather bag that looked, from the way he was holding it, to be very heavy.

She was just about to say something more when, in what seemed like slow motion, Tom's hand came towards her and clamped down firmly over her mouth. Terror overtook reason. She wanted to scream but his grip was too secure. All she could think of was that this was the end and Elizabeth was upstairs, blissfully unaware of the drama below.

Elizabeth!

FORTY-EIGHT

Hannah's heart was pounding so wildly she thought she would explode. *Oh my God, she thought, Elizabeth.*

Her protests were muffled. She struggled to no effect and it was several minutes before she realised that Tom's hold on her was more of an embrace than anything else. She managed to wriggle around so she could look up into his eyes.

He was smiling.

She couldn't believe her eyes. He was actually grinning at her. The other man who had pushed past them, came out of the sitting room with a nod in Tom's direction. Tom guided her into the empty room and onto the sofa.

Without loosening his hold on her, he bent forward and kissed her forehead. "Don't look so worried," he whispered into her hair. "Graham's a mate of mine. He's checking the house for bugs. This room's ok now, but don't scream at me when I let go, okay?"

Hannah, saucer-eyed, nodded.

Tom slowly removed his hand. "Sorry to frighten you like that." He was master of the understatement.

"Frighten me? You nearly gave me a heart attack." Hannah flopped back against the cushions and closed her eyes for a moment. When she opened them again, her breathing was still ragged and the room was swimming.

Tom forced her head between her knees, lightly stroking the back of her neck. He didn't speak. Her breathing slowly returned to near normal and she sat up just as the other man walked into the room.

"This is Graham Stradan, special effects man." Hannah was none the wiser. "Hannah Weybridge," Tom concluded the introductions.

"Sorry to barge in on you like this, Hannah, unannounced," said Graham, "but we had reason to believe you'd been bugged. I found these –" he held out two tiny devices – "under the phones. Everything else is clean," he said to Tom.

Hannah opened her mouth and closed it again.

"Has anybody been here from Telecom recently?" Graham asked.

Hannah shook her head, still stunned by what was happening.

"Oh well, they probably let themselves in when you were out." Tom looked across at Graham. "Professional job?"

"Top hole." Hannah didn't understand the impact of those two words, but when he smiled at her in an attempt to be reassuring, she realised just how serious his expression was.

"I don't understand any of this," said Hannah. They were sitting next to each other on the settee. Both cradled glasses of scotch. Graham had departed after a swift cup of coffee.

"I'm afraid I can't tell you much more now. It's out of my hands, I'm off the case." Tom drank deeply from his glass. His face was grim. "As soon as I handed over your evidence, the ranks closed and I was told to take some leave." There was a lack of bitterness in his tone that surprised her.

Hannah studied his face. The frown lines now seemed deeper than the laughter ones. He had the appearance of someone who had been on a long, grueling journey, only to find he had to turn back just before reaching his destination. Or did he?

Although Hannah couldn't explain why, she was sure Tom was holding out on her. Maybe it had something to do with the Official Secrets Act. Tom Jordan was evidently more that the BT police inspector he claimed to be.

They had turned on the television for the ten o'clock news. Robert Bowldon's death was the lead item. The IRA was suspected.

"Nearer home more like," commented Tom dryly.

Hannah turned to him, but she didn't want to ask what he meant. Each possibility was too appalling to contemplate. "And what about Tony Vitello?"

"Well," Tom paused to take Hannah's hand. "Princess – Caroline – had definitely been in his flat recently. Forensic proved that before we were called off. Whether she went there willingly or not, we'll never know."

Hannah blinked rapidly to disperse the tears that were flooding her eyes. She sipped her whisky.

"My guess – and it's only a surmise – is that Caroline contacted Vitello and she did go to his flat. It makes no difference now. What is probable is that Vitello found out about the notebooks and tried his hand at blackmail. But he was out of his league. He was rapidly disposed of and Princess was taken back to the – clinic." His voice betrayed the contempt he felt for that establishment.

"So what will happen now?"

"The clinic's been closed and sealed up. At the moment, security is tighter there than at Buck House. What they'll find in there, we'll probably never know."

"I don't think I want to," Hannah said quietly.

Tom glanced at her and took her free hand. "No, I don't suppose you do."

They were silent, each with their own thoughts. "And what about him?" The thought that the perpetrator of all this had sat next to her in this house, in her home, made her feel guilty by association.

Tom shrugged. "Oh someone will probably find some irregularity with Dr Gerry Lacon's immigration papers and he'll be discretely deported back to South Africa, where I understand, he has every reason not to feel too safe."

"Well, I don't suppose he'll get what he deserves." Hannah ran her fingers through her hair and could feel the whisky having a relaxing effect on her.

"I wouldn't be too sure of that," was all Tom would say.

"And the others?"

"Who knows? Who bloody knows?"

"Well, Robert Bowldon's met his end."

"Yes." Tom's expression was grim.

Hannah was silent for a moment and then asked the question that had been bothering her ever since the arrival of Tom and Graham. "What about me?" In the face of Caroline's suffering, it sounded to her own ears amazingly selfish. "Am I safe?"

For a long moment Tom didn't reply. Hannah could feel her stomach tensing. Tom looked her straight in the eye. "I think so, Hannah."

She could sense the breath easing out of her body. She did trust Tom. She had to trust somebody, but was his thinking she'd be safe, enough, she asked herself bitterly.

"Too many people know now. If anything happened to you... well they couldn't gag us all could they?" Tom gave a hollow laugh. "I should think the powers that be will make damn sure you are all right, if you see what I mean."

Hannah wasn't quite sure that she did, but that was probably due to the whisky and the way Tom pulled her to him and covered her unprotesting mouth with his own, just before Elizabeth staked her own noisy claim to her mother's attention.

FORTY-NINE

Hannah mounted the three steps to the lectern. Her legs leaden, she could see her hands shaking as she placed the sheet of paper in front of her and gripped the wooden frame to steady herself.

She glanced up. There were few people there and she knew that neither of Caroline's parents would be attending the funeral. Which was why she had been asked to say a few words. You could hardly call it a eulogy.

"Many of you knew her as Princess and that's who she was when I first met and interviewed her. But after she turned up on my doorstep, badly beaten up and in need of a refuge, she became Caroline to me…"

Her voice broke. She looked up and saw a row of police officers in uniform at the back. Tom Jordan was there, along with his sergeant and the WPC. Each of them looked sombre. But she had the feeling that they weren't exactly looking at her. They were taking stock of who else was in the congregation.

Hannah spied Jaynie and Marti, both very respectably dressed in black. The latter stared at her as though willing Hannah to go on. She smiled tremulously. There were a couple of other people, one or two looked like tramps and a man with a shock of grey hair, who, Hannah had noticed earlier, walked with a distinct limp.

Hannah's gaze returned to her sheet of paper.

"Caroline spent most of the last few weeks of her life living with me and I grew to know more of her background. She hadn't had any advantages in life and the cards were definitely stacked against her. But she didn't complain or rant against fate. What she did try to do was seek justice for her friends and this led ultimately to her own death.

"I didn't know Caroline well enough to understand what she was planning. Unfortunately, to me she was irritating and unpredictable – in short, a typical teenager who sadly had witnessed more of life than she ever should have. She knew too much and that knowledge led to her death."

Hannah swallowed hard. The words in front of her blurred. She blinked rapidly. Her knuckles were white as she clung onto the lectern.

"I am so sorry that I didn't manage to keep her safe and that I have been unable to expose her killers – yet." The last word was little more than a breath.

Hannah turned to the coffin. "Caroline, Princess, your friends mourn your loss. Perhaps one day we'll find a way to bring the perpetrators of your murder to justice."

The priest looked increasingly uncomfortable. She glared at him.

She laid a small posy of flowers picked from her garden that morning on the coffin and walked back to her seat.

Tom Jordan noted that one of the tramps left very quickly.

The priest said a closing prayer and as heads were bowed, pushed the button for the curtains to close as the coffin disappeared, to the stains of Whitney Houston singing "I Will Always Love You", from, Hannah had discovered, Caroline's favourite film, *The Bodyguard.*

◊ ◊ ◊

Outside the crematorium, Marti hugged Hannah. "Just be careful," she said so that only Hannah could hear. She and Jaynie turned towards the man with a limp. "Come on Sam, we'll all go back together. Stop off and have a drink, eh?"

Jaynie and Marti linked arms with the man and they headed off.

"Can we give you a lift back, Hannah?" Tom Jordan, looking so different and rather forbidding in uniform, stood before her.

Hannah noticed they hadn't used a squad car. She felt a deep, deep weariness and despair. She had been rendered powerless.

She nodded. "Thanks."

◊ ◊ ◊

A few days later, Hannah's eyes were drawn to the obituary columns where a familiar name sprang out at her.

Roger Daintly!

Roger Daintly had won an Oscar for his performance as an aging gay in a low-budget movie that had surprised everyone by capturing the imagination of the cinema-going public. The film became a blockbuster and its star a cult hero.

Roger Daintly.

Daintly's name had been on Marti's list of men attending Lacon's clinic. Hannah leafed back through the paper, but could find no report of his death. She rescued the previous day's newspaper, which she'd been trying to read in bed before sleep had defeated her attempts, from the waste-paper basket.

She found what she was looking for on page three. Two column inches devoted to the death of one of Britain's greatest actors. Apparently, he'd been discovered dead in his bed by his cleaning lady, an empty bottle of sleeping pills on the floor. His GP confirmed that he'd been treating him for depression and insomnia for some time. He thought it possible that the actor had overdosed himself by mistake – perhaps waking and taking more tablets, forgetting he'd already taken some.

I've heard that one before, thought Hannah. *I wonder if it was really suicide?* Had someone helped him on his way?

Two down and how many more to go?

The third death a few days later was the Bishop of Essex who had succumbed to a massive heart attack. God striking back?

And the opposition MP Carl Douglas had made a surprising announcement that he was to retire from his seat to spend more time with his wife and family. Maybe justice was being done.

Hannah didn't know whether she felt safer or in more danger. It sent a shiver of apprehension down her spine.

One thing was certain – she needed a break. A visit to her parents' new home in France was long overdue and now seemed like a very opportune time.

FIFTY

It was dark. The nights were drawing in now. Hannah carried Elizabeth still strapped into her car seat into the hall and dragged her suitcase after her. Picking Elizabeth up, still asleep in her chair, she walked into the sitting room and switched on a lamp.

"Welcome home."

The male voice made Hannah spin on her heels. She almost collapsed in terror when she saw Gerry Lacon sitting in an armchair, smiling.

"What the ..."

"You didn't think I'd let you get away scot free, did you? Come, come, that would have been careless of me." The smile disappeared. "You have ruined everything, you silly woman. Sit down," he ordered.

She stood rooted to the spot.

Hannah felt all hope drain from her.

"Some talented men have lost their lives because you just couldn't keep your stupid nose out of things that were none of your business. Because of you, my marriage is over. Because of

278   **DANCERS IN THE WIND**

you, I have had all my financial assets frozen. All because you just had to befriend a stinking whore. Sit down."

Hannah had backed to the settee and collapsed onto it.

"Why are you here? You've no right to break into my house…"

"Oh I didn't break in, I got someone else to do that for me." His smile froze Hannah's heart. Bile rose in her throat. *Think!* She told herself. *Think!*

It was then that she noticed the small gun in Gerry Lacon's hand and she thought she would faint. She stood to reach her sleeping child.

"Sit down." The order was spoken quietly but the menace was implicit. Hannah now knew what was meant by blood draining from someone. She didn't have an ounce of strength. Then she looked at Elizabeth – there was no way…

"I've been pondering what I should do to pay you back."

"Please –"

"Shut up." The genial façade, if it as ever there, had completely vanished. "I thought, what could I do to Ms Hannah Weybridge to give her a taste of her own medicine?" He waved the gun in an arc. "Fortunately my off-shore assets haven't been unearthed and I can still get – unpalatable – jobs done or covered up for me."

That smile again. Hannah wondered what her chances would be if she just threw herself at him. There was an ornament on the chest of drawers next to where he was sitting. If she aimed for that then hit him for all she was worth…

Somewhere there was a whisper of a noise she couldn't place or identify. Were her potential killers in the house already?

Gerry Lacon looked at her with his supercilious smile. "Don't worry, we've been through all your documents and files and we've added a few of our own…"

Hannah couldn't think what on earth he meant. She'd gone

from cold to hot and now clammy. She had never felt so alone or petrified in her life.

That noise again. Gerry lifted the gun and pointed it at Elizabeth. The loud retort synchronised with her agonised scream as she launched her body across the room to protect her child "Nooooo…"

And then the room was full of men in what looked like riot gear and voices shouting to get down. Hannah fell to the floor and crawled to Elizabeth who was crying but amazingly didn't seem to be harmed in any way. With hands almost unable to function, Hannah unstrapped her and clutched the infant to her, sobbing soundlessly.

It wasn't until she felt someone lifting her gently and saying repeatedly: "It's over, Hannah, it's over," that she opened her eyes and stared into the face of Tom Jordan.

"I think I'm going to be sick." Hannah moved to one side and retched until there was nothing more. She was aware that Tom was holding back her hair and realised that he'd taken Elizabeth from her and was talking quietly to someone.

"Hello Hannah, I'm Pete, a paramedic. I just need you to focus on me for a few minutes…"

Pete shone a light into her eyes, took her blood pressure and temperature. Then gave her something to drink. "It's just some rehydrating salts to make you feel a bit better."

A blanket had been wrapped around her shoulders, and then Elizabeth was smiling up into her eyes. *She's alive. She isn't hurt.* The words echoed in her mind before they were led out of the house and into a waiting police car.

EPILOGUE

Over dinner a week later, Tom and Hannah compared notes about their respective holidays. It had been an attempt to return to real life – to a life before Caroline.

"I need space and I need to put some distance between myself and all that has happened," Hannah had said three weeks before.

Now, Tom wondered if she'd go off again. It had taken several conversations to calm Hannah's growing sense of paranoia. How had they known about Gerry Lacon's plans and if they had known, why hadn't they interceded sooner?

Tom had looked appalled. The armed back-up unit had been cancelled at the last minute. He and two colleagues had been listening in, when they heard the order.

They had managed to scramble together a second unit, but they had lost precious minutes.

The gunshot Hannah had heard came from an SO19 officer who blasted the gun from Gerry Lacon's hand.

Lacon had been deported to South Africa with the minimum of publicity.

Hannah was furious. He had been going to shoot her daughter in front of her and they had let him go. What Hannah didn't know was that he was arrested on arrival and charged with murder and crimes against the state. He was destined for a very long prison sentence.

There was so much that Tom couldn't tell her – she knew why but it didn't make it any easier to accept. Emotionally. What she did know was that he had been working under cover. But that also wasn't up for discussion.

"So, what will you do now?" Tom asked as he poured more wine.

Hannah sipped her wine. "Well, thanks to The News I won't have money worries for a while, so I'm going to write that novel I've always promised myself."

"And us?" He waited for the answer, his face a picture of uncertainty. He looked younger, eager.

Hannah sighed. "I still need time and space –" She grinned. "I'd like to work on that too."

Tom raised his glass and smiled.

Death's Silent Judgement, Anne Coates' thrilling sequel to *Dancers in the Wind*, will be published Spring, 2017 by Urbane Publications.

You can enjoy an EXCLUSIVE glimpse of the opening chapter ...

ONE

The first thing that hit her was the smell and it made her gag. A mixture of odours, chemical and the metallic tang of blood, combined in an unholy alliance. An alliance which threatened to make the contents of her stomach evacuate in protest. She held a handkerchief to her face and tried to control her breathing – and the desperate urge to run out of the room. As her eyes became accustomed to the gloom, her glance took in the chaos, the overturned chair, the broken glass, the contents of Liz's briefcase scattered across the floor and then her brain registered what her heart had cried out against – Liz's inert body draped across the make-shift dentist's chair.

She made herself walk the four paces which brought her to the body and the certain knowledge that Liz Rayman was dead.

◊ ◊ ◊

"Right, let's go through it one more time. You arrived here at 6.50pm. There was no one around when you entered the church and you saw no one as you made your way downstairs to the room she was using?"

"No." Hannah Weybridge sipped the glass of water that had just been handed to her by a young constable. "I mean yes, that's right." She could still taste the bile she had brought up, vomiting by the steps outside, just after she had phoned the police. Thank heavens for mobiles, she wouldn't have trusted her legs to carry her to a phone box. She shuddered. What was the point of all this repeated questioning? It must be obvious – even to the police sergeant sitting at the other side of the table in the vestry – that she wasn't the murderer.

"How long had you known Miss Rayman?"

Had. Hannah hated the man for his use of the past tense. What an insensitive pig. "About ten years," she replied quietly. Forever, said her heart. Liz had been a real soul mate. They had met at a New Year's Eve party given by a mutual friend who had a small flat in Fulham. Everyone had seemed to know everyone else – except Hannah and Liz who had gravitated towards each other. They had both come to the party alone but neither showed any interest in the spare males who hovered nearby then decided to try their luck elsewhere. That night they'd talked about books and books led them to the theatre that turned out to be a passion with them both. They toasted the New Year in champagne and parted in the early hours.

Liz had rung a few days later with an invitation to see the new Ackbourn play. Their friendship had flourished ever since through their various relationships with men and Liz's decision to take a sabbatical from her dentistry practice and join a medical charity in Africa. A choice Hannah had found both unfathomable and hurtful. She had been away for the birth of Hannah's daughter whom she'd named after Liz.

"Ten years," she repeated in a whisper. She shuddered. The cold had penetrated her heavy coat and scarf. Bone-chilling. The shock of what she had seen was mind-numbing. Her hand began shaking so much that the water spilled from the paper cup she was holding. She put it down on the table in front of her.

"And what were you doing here this evening?" The sergeant's eyes, with crow's-feet at the outer corners suggesting a happier side to him, were bloodshot from tiredness or perhaps ill health. His mousey hair had outgrown its cut and curled slightly over his collar. But there was nothing mousey about the way he looked at her. More rat-like.

Hannah wanted to scream. She'd already told them what she was doing there: she had arranged to meet Liz at the "mission" as she called it, before going to dinner. "She had something important to tell me," and she didn't want to say it in the the nearby Italian restaurant where the tables were set so close together you could almost hear the other diners breathing let alone confiding secrets. Hannah had been intrigued both to hear Liz's news and to see where her friend worked one day a week, giving free dental treatment and advice to the down and outs who inhabited the environs of Waterloo. The Bullring. Cardboard City.

Hannah, who knew the area well from her IPC Magazines days, had walked past St John's countless times but had never been inside the church. To her it's Grecian pillars were nothing more than a landmark on the south side of Waterloo Bridge. She was curious that Liz should be practising there. Apparently the priest ran a soup kitchen and, when he'd met Liz at some fund-raising function linked to the charity work she'd been doing in Somalia, had prevailed upon her good nature and inveigled her into opening a walk-in clinic.

Some clinic, thought Hannah. Liz had to carry all her instruments and supplies with her and had to do all her sterilising back at her Barbican practice. As she never had a dental nurse with her, she used to dictate notes about the patient's dental condition into a small dictaphone.

"The dictaphone!"

"I'm sorry Miss?"

"Look for her dictaphone! Liz always used it to dictate her notes maybe it'll hold some clue, maybe the murderer's voice..." Hannah had half risen from her chair but seeing the sergeant's patronising smile that was really more of a grimace, she sank back down and rested her head in her hands. Any minute now she would wake up and this awful interview would would fade from her consciousness.

Hannah closed her eyes and then opened them quickly to chase away the image of her friend's lifeless body, her throat slashed, her eyes staring out of a face which looked remarkably composed for someone who had just been brutally murdered. It suddenly occurred to Hannah that if she had arrived any earlier she might have been a witness – a dead witness an inner voice corrected. For why should whoever killed Liz leave Hannah alive to tell the tale?

"I'm sorry," said Hannah as she just managed to turn away in time to throw up into a waste paper basket.

"I'll get a squad car to take you home."

Ashen faced, Hannah nodded her thanks. Within minutes she was being ushered through the church by a young policewoman. As they passed the room that had been Liz's surgery, Hannah took in the blaze of lights and a photographer shooting the dead body from every conceivable angle. Hannah shuddered. There's no dignity and certainly no privacy in death, she thought. At least not in a violent one.

The icy night air was like a slap in the face. A small crowd had gathered by the steps leading up to the church behind the police tape. Two policemen opened up a passage for Hannah and her companion to pass through. Hannah was aware of a murmur then a shout.

"Hey, Lady, what the hell's going on in there?"

Hannah glanced in the the direction the voice had come from and her eyes were held by an imposing figure that seemed to stand a head above the crowd. His mane of white hair was brushed away from his lined and craggy face and he stood proud despite the fact that his clothes were rags and he carried his home in a battered suitcase.

Hannah shook her head, grateful for the steadying arm of the policewoman. As the car set off she looked back to see that the man seemed to be staring after her. Perhaps he was one of Liz's patients. Silently the tears rolled down her face and as she tried to brush them away with the back of her hand. The policewoman handed her an extra-strong mint.

"I always carry them with me now." She smiled and Hannah noticed the shadows beneath her eyes. "I don't think I'll ever get used to it."

"I hope you don't," said Hannah, wishing she could rid herself of the sickening image of her friend's dead body and of the question resounding in her head. Why Liz? Why?

ACKNOWLEDGEMENTS

It is wonderful when a writer finds a dynamic publisher who is enthusiastic about her manuscript. I was so fortunate to find such a one in Matthew Smith and it has been a joy to work with him and Urbane Publishers.

Dancers in the Wind was a long time in gestation. First written many years ago, then put away in a drawer and forgotten but not quite... Rereading it one afternoon I realised I still wanted to write this story and so began a long process of rewriting, editing and changing until this version was achieved.

In its first incarnation, my friend Fiona Jack read each chapter virtually as it came off the printer and kept reading... I wonder what she will make of it now? My thanks also to Elizabeth Bull and Sue O'Neill who were enthusiastic in their praise for this version. I am grateful also to the support of Twitter friends especially Charlotte Sing and Debs Ramsdale who took the time to give me their views and to Debbie Scholes who proofread before submission.

If it takes a village to raise a child, the same could be said for creating a fictional world and I am enormously blessed with supportive friends who have helped me in so many ways not least by giving me quirks and characteristics that I have sometimes used for my characters.

My own daughter, Olivia, has grown up during the period of this book's gestation and is a constant source of inspiration and love and it is to her that I dedicate this book.

For most of her working life in publishing, Anne has had a foot in both camps as a writer and an editor, moving from book publishing to magazines and then freelancing in both.

Having edited both fiction and narrative non-fiction, Anne has also had short stories published in a variety of magazines including *Bella and Candis* and is the author of seven non-fiction books.

Born in Clapham, Anne returned to London after graduating and has remained there ever since. In an attempt to climb out of her comfort zone, Anne has twice "trod the boards" – as Prince Bourgrelas in *Ubu Roi* when a student and more recently as a nun in a local murder mystery production. She also sings periodically in a local church choir and is relieved when she begins and finishes at the same time – though not necessarily on the same note – as everyone else. Needless to say, Anne will not be giving up her day job as an editor and writer.

Telling stories is Anne's first love and nearly all her short fiction as well as Dancers in The Wind began with a real event followed by a "what if …" That is also the case with the two prize-winning 99Fiction.net stories: Codewords and Eternal Love.

Anne is currently working on *Death's Silent Judgement*, the sequel to *Dancers in the Wind*.

Urbane Publications is dedicated to
developing new author voices, and publishing
fiction and non-fiction that challenges, thrills and
fascinates.

From page-turning novels to innovative
reference books, our goal is to publish what
YOU want to read.

Find out more at
urbanepublications.com